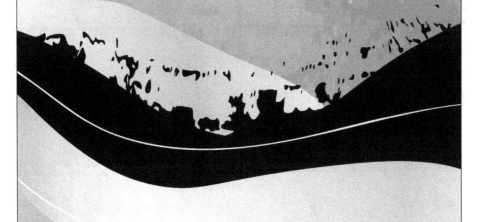

HOMER'S GRACE

A NOVEL

BY
CHESLEY RICHARDS

Wisdom House Books

HOMER'S GRACE

Copyright © 2022 Chesley Richards
All rights reserved.

No part of this publication may be reproduced, stored in a retrieval system, or transmitted in any way by any means, electronic, mechanical, photocopy, recording or otherwise without the prior permission of the author except as provided by USA copyright law.

The opinions expressed by the author are not necessarily those of Wisdom House Books, Inc.

Published by Wisdom House Books, Inc.
Chapel Hill, North Carolina 27517 USA
www.wisdomhousebooks.com

Wisdom House Books is committed to excellence in the publishing industry.

Book design copyright © 2022 by Wisdom House Books, Inc. All rights reserved.

Cover and Interior Design by Ted Ruybal

Published in the United States of America

Paperback ISBN: 979-8-9861008-0-7
LCCN: 2022914319

1. FIC016000 | FICTION / Humorous / General
2. FIC031000 | FICTION / Thrillers / General
3. FIC002000 | FICTION / Action & Adventure

First Edition

25 24 23 22 21 20 / 10 9 8 7 6 5 4 3 2 1

This novel's story and characters are fictitious.

Real institutions or organizations are mentioned in some instances, but the characters and activities involved are wholly imaginary.

Grace, Georgia is an imaginary town.

TABLE OF CONTENTS

	Acknowledgements	vii
1	It's About the Land and the Legacy	1
2	A Llama-Inspired Fiasco Begins	15
3	The Blue Mustang	27
4	A Terrorist Attack	33
5	Homer Restores Order—Sort of	45
6	Super Athlete and Intrepid Businessman, Alvin Teabody	59
7	A Background Investigation Begins	67
8	The Summer of 1963	75
9	Decisions and Dinner	79
10	A New Venture	93
11	Biltmore	99
12	New pursuits	111
13	The Story About the Swiss Man	115
14	Alvin, I Have Another Proposition	119

15	Breakfast at the Cafe	133
16	Manly Conversations	141
17	November 1963	157
18	Good News and Bad News	161
19	The Montcliffs	165
20	Construction and Celebration	169
21	Away in Switzerland	177
22	The Year Was 1307	195
23	Archaeology in Grace	199
24	Dr. Emilia Gisler	209
25	A New Sheriff	213
26	A Visit to the Cave	219
27	Morning in Grace	229
28	Final Revelations	243
	About the Author	247

ACKNOWLEDGEMENTS

I would like to thank Frank Dilley, Ed Baker, John Matthews, and Dana Pitts for providing both critiques and support for some of my early ideas and drafts of this story. They gave me the courage to pursue, seriously, my lifelong desire to tell stories.

Thank you to Janie Mills who edited my first draft and who guided me, challenged me, and gave me such wonderful support and encouragement in my stumbling effort to become an author.

Thank you to my wife, Sophia, and my daughter, Ana, for your honesty, enthusiasm, support, and unconditional love. I would not be here without you.

CHAPTER 1

IT'S ABOUT THE LAND AND THE LEGACY

On that fine spring Sunday morning in April, Grace, Georgia, was peaceful and quiet. As with many small southern towns, a Sunday morning was still sacred—going to church or just sleeping in after a wild Saturday night. No lawnmowers, no shopping till noon, and no yelling. But, when the clock struck noon and church was out, things heated up a bit. The Longfellows enjoyed the scents of jasmine and magnolia, moderate humidity, and receding pollen counts that morning. Until a few minutes after noon.

"Carl! Homer Pitts is on the front porch sitting in your wicker rocking chair!" the tall, acerbic Lula Bell Longfellow boomed out. "What are you going to do about it?" Carl Longfellow sat motionless in the oak-paneled den in his weathered, leather armchair with a nice breeze blowing over his shoulder while watching his Sunday afternoon TV programs.

"Okay," Carl said after a few moments.

Lula Bell threw up her hands in disgust. She spun around, facing the front porch, muttering obscenities. "Homer, please, not today. No whining today." She needed a break on the Lord's day.

"Lula Bell, thank you so much, dear. But I am here to see your husband, the man of the house. Whoopee!" said the politely sarcastic and diminutive Homer whose high-pitched, squeaky drawl could make a Sunday school teacher cuss. His spring attire was a light blue striped seersucker suit, white button-down shirt, Panama straw hat, and pink bowtie. His nearly bald head, with wisps of still golden fine hair, shined brightly in the noon day sunshine penetrating the porch. His face was round, as were his brown, horn-rimmed, retro 1960s glasses.

"And I would appreciate it if you would get him out here right now!" Homer added, smiling.

"He doesn't want to see you. So, be gone with your Cheshire cat-grinning self, will you?" Lula Bell said in a rhetorical brush-off. She promptly strode back inside to fetch Carl.

Finally, after a long while, Carl stood up, stretched, and walked to the porch. Carl sported a comfortable navy-blue sweater, a full head of curly white hair, and the tanned face of a semi-retired patrician lawyer and real estate broker who played golf every other day. Quite tall and possessing a mellow baritone voice, Carl towered as he sat down in the chair opposite Homer. On this occasion, like many, Carl was forced to take the guest chair. Homer sat in the fan-shaped wicker chair marked with a red wooden sign, "Carl's chair. Don't sit here if you aren't Carl." Homer generally ignored the instruction.

"Homer, why are you here on a Sunday?" Carl asked.

Carl's presence tended to bring out the chihuahua-like bark in Homer.

"Carl, you know."

"No, I don't. Tell me."

IT'S ABOUT THE LAND AND THE LEGACY

In 1980, Carl was Grace's mayor when Homer's papa and brothers sold some land. The property transaction was Carl's first act as a new, young mayor. Homer's family split up the money, but both Homer and his mama were left out. Carl was intimately aware of the circumstances of Homer's complaint, and yet, he still liked to hear Homer's latest angle.

"The land, Carl. But it won't change anything," Homer said petulantly.

"Then why did you come?" Carl questioned.

"Because something has to be done. We have to set right for eternity what was not set right in life," Homer repeated after so many years of saying the same thing over and over. The land was originally his mama's, but it was part of a poor white family's dowry to get his mama married off. Her much older, previously-married husband and sons took the land and then the proceeds from its sale.

"Homer, you know that the courthouse, town hall, sheriff's office, and the Grace Comprehensive School are on that land. It's not your land anymore. It's Courthouse Square, and it belongs to the town of Grace."

"My mama and I were cheated."

"Homer, the town paid your family $41,231.55 back then for the land."

"How did you remember that?" Homer said as he feigned shock at Carl's recollection.

"You have been here, with this complaint, many times," Carl reminded Homer.

"Well, Carl, I still believe they cheated Mama and me out of the land. Yes, legally, it was Daddy's, but that's beside the point. It wasn't just."

"Homer, when you get paid a fair price, it isn't stealing. And the legal deed was in his name."

In the South, land represents more than dirt, grass, and trees. It's part of your identity. "Where are you from?" is right up there with "Who's your daddy and mama?" as an essential questions. Homer didn't need the money or the land, specifically. But he was interested in justice and legacy.

"Oh, my dear mama," Homer exclaimed, "and those no-good Pitts. They took her land!"

Homer generally broke down into tears at this point in the conversation. Usually, he asked for a handkerchief or a glass of sweet, iced tea. Today, Homer's tears were abundant. And abundant tears usually meant sweet tea along with an approaching low-pressure front and lots of rain.

"What will it be, sweet tea or handkerchief?" Lula Bell reentered the scene so suddenly, her voice so loud and fierce, that Homer nearly fell out of Carl's chair. He grabbed his chest to emphasize the point. Lula Bell stood with the screen door open, one foot on the porch and the other on the hardwood floor of her elegantly-appointed living room.

"Lula Bell, that voice of yours. Oh my! It's still as frightening as it was in the third grade when I first laid eyes on you, you Amazonian warrior princess!" Homer paused for effect, letting his little three-word description sink in a bit. "Sweet tea, with two cubes of ice, a little lemon, and a sprig of fresh mint would be delightful," Homer smiled.

Typical Homer. It started with tears of agony, enough to make you weepy too, and generally ended with a mischievous smile and a specific request. Carl took it all in and thought a bit before he spoke again. And he waited on the tea to come before delivering his latest news.

IT'S ABOUT THE LAND AND THE LEGACY

There were a few things Carl knew. Homer left Grace to become an unlikely icon of New York fashion. At 19, he arrived in New York City and lived for a while in Greenwich Village. He went to Columbia, and on weekends, he talked his way into Studio 54, using his resemblance to Truman Capote to sneak in. He got to know people, designed, and eventually became the talk among the fashion houses. A couple of trips to Milan and Paris followed. He accumulated a small fortune giving advice and writing articles about people, tastes, passions, and fashion ideas. He listened patiently to the deepest, darkest confessions from his celebrity pals and kept their confidences. After several years in the limelight and the right circles, he was finally someone important. Then in 1995, in his mid-thirties, at the height of his fame and wealth, he was summoned home to the small town that formed him, despite the prejudices and neuroses and small-mindedness he escaped. He returned for Mama. Her cancer was taking her away piece by piece.

Homer kept his pain to himself and focused his energies on giving Mama the best comfort he could—that included elevating the culture in Grace. That was something Mama always wanted for Grace. She had once been to New York City, and she liked the culture there. So, Homer wanted her to have a little before she left this life. For the library, he contributed the entire Harvard Classics and Greatest Books of the Western World collections. He sponsored the spring concert and July 4th jubilee for the Grace Comprehensive School Band. He helped struggling families make decorative art to sell to out-of-towners who came to the newly-opened antique mall on weekends. And he helped with set design and costumes for the little playhouse he started for the weekends in the now reopened, formerly abandoned movie theatre at

Courthouse Square. Homer started the mall and reopened the theatre by convincing an Atlanta bank that opening closed properties could make them a little money and raise the property values. He gave prom fashion advice to the teenage girls and gave the boys similar advice on how to compliment the girls with a matching wardrobe. He started a reading club attended by forty ladies where he gave lectures on his friends' books, To Kill a Mockingbird and In Cold Blood, sprinked with personal gossip about the authors. Mama was tickled pink to watch all the society ladies fall all over themselves asking questions to which her Homer had clever replies. Homer instituted so many other culture upgrades. By the time Mama died, Homer had put down roots again. Generally, he was happy, but one thing continued to rub him the wrong way. He wanted to right the wrong done to him by his father and stepbrothers. But, it wasn't the same as having land that once belonged to his mama's family.

Sometimes, Homer's emotions about the whole situation got the better of him. He conducted a protest march around Courthouse Square on those occasions with a bullhorn shouting, "I was robbed!" Sheriff Meeks would walk out to warn Homer he might have to go to jail. Homer wasn't keen on spending time in jail.

Roaches—more accurately, the giant Palmetto bugs endemic to musty old Southern buildings. Homer was particularly frightened of flying ones attracted to light since the jailer kept the lights on all night, like Motel Six. So, that's where Homer drew the line—no more jail time for him. Sheriff Meeks fined Homer instead. It was a deal that satisfied Homer and helped the Sheriff meet his payroll. Sometimes though, Homer's voice carried down to Main Street Christian Church of Grace.

IT'S ABOUT THE LAND AND THE LEGACY

"That man needs to be taught a lesson," Reverend J. Leland Jackson told Sheriff Meeks. "Interrupting the peace in our town is not okay. Even with the window shut and the air conditioner running, I can still hear him in my office. I can't write my sermon on Christian love when I am so irritated."

Sheriff Meeks finally gave Homer a three-hour jail sentence to satisfy the reverend. In response, Homer screamed, begged, cajoled, fidgeted, writhed, and produced so much chaos outside on the sidewalk that a crowd gathered. Even the school kids on the playground ran over to see the fun. His Agapovs supported him in the ordeal, but Homer wouldn't let the Agapovs go with him to jail. He wouldn't have it. He said it would be like reliving the "Gulag Archipelago" for them, even though the Agapovs were never in a Soviet labor camp.

The Agapovs were Homer's domestic staff. When Homer moved back to Grace, the textile mills had all closed down. People were out of work, and real estate bottomed out. The family who owned the mills were long departed to Naples, Florida, while most mill workers retired to their living rooms, La-Z-Boy recliners, and unemployment checks. But that left the mill owner's mansion in a state of decline, written off as a loss and vacated. After Mama died, Homer bought the mansion. He spent a substantial amount of his small fortune to purchase and get the old, run-down estate back in shape. It would be a dignified place to live, he thought. Six thousand square feet to renovate and a new Olympic-sized swimming pool to add. Then he purchased the two adjoining vacant farms, creating a three-hundred-acre estate complete with a mansion, small mountain, meandering stream, pastureland, woodlands, and barns. He had successfully converted most of his fortune into the land he owned. But, he still had publishing royalties to cover his needs.

On his first night there, lying alone in his antique Hepplewhite poster canopy bed, Homer realized that one man on such a grand estate would be uncivilized. Homer, a fan of Tolstoy, Dostoevsky, and Pushkin, realized that he needed a Russian family to join him on the estate. So, Homer's blessing from a loving God was the Agapovs, who answered his Russian newspaper ad for "an opportunity to live with royalty." The "with" was not accurate since Homer had no royal titles because the U.S. constitution prohibits royal titles in Article 1 Section 9 Clause 8, which Homer knew since he wrote an eighth-grade essay on the necessity of revising that clause for specific worthy individuals. But Homer thought "with" sounded better than "like," so he stuck with it.

Homer engaged in a bit of international diplomacy and some bribes to eventually get the Agapovs to Grace. Vladimir, the father, was a tall man with broad shoulders, a long salt-and-pepper beard, and big hands and feet. Trained as a mechanical engineer, Vladimir quickly rebuilt and renovated the mansion as Homer's estate manager. Valentina, the mama, was a full-figured mountain of loving motherliness. She cooked and cleaned and sang and generally hung on every word of her new employer. Then there were the nine well-behaved children: Mikhail, Anya, Tanya, Masha, Boris, Ekaterina, Ludmilla, Sonya, and little Sasha. Mikhail was eighteen when they came to Grace, and Sasha was four. And the others were somewhere in between. Each had a chore or two, and all received art, music, and fashion lessons from Mister Homer.

IT'S ABOUT THE LAND AND THE LEGACY

Back to Homer's protest marches. The Agapovs enthusiastically followed Homer, banging tambourines and singing "We Shall Overcome" just as he taught them. The result was a beautiful a cappella harmony characteristic of chants in a Russian Orthodox Church. They loved Homer so much that they even changed their name to honor him. Or, more rightly, lengthened their name to Agapov-Pitts. But for some reason, the townspeople thought it meant "apricot pits," which turn into cyanide in your intestines. A few hysterics thought that the Agapov-Pitts might be a family of assassins. After a few weeks, the Agapov-Pitts went back to just Agapov to settle things down. Some of the townsfolk believed that Homer started the rumor to make the town fear him. But most folks didn't think Homer was capable of something like that.

Despite his spending, Homer was still modestly wealthy from a small-town perspective. So he spent money on others. Homer's passion in life was righting wrongs, correcting deficiencies, and finally being accepted and respected in the place from which he had come. They say, "you can't go home again," but Homer had. He endured taunts, jokes, and general abuse for being different and a little outlandish. But all Homer wanted was to be accepted and, maybe, loved and admired a little. Even his years in New York City were a struggle for respect for the folks at home to be proud of him.

Carl considered all this as he thought about how best to tell Homer.

"Thank you, Miss Lula Bell. Just perfect," Homer said as he took a sip of the iced tea with lemon and mint—all fresh.

"Homer, do you realize that this is the fortieth anniversary of the land transfer?" Carl asked.

"No, uh, I didn't realize that," Homer replied cautiously. He did know that but wasn't sure where Carl was going with this, so he feigned ignorance.

"Well, you are not going to get the land. Let's put an end to that." After so long, Carl was ready to be blunt and move on. "But, I think we have something that might just be more appropriate, if you'll hear me out."

"Okay, Carl. Let's hear it before I go on a hunger strike along with my marches!" Homer was ready to endure.

"The town council met this week, and we voted unanimously to recognize you for your lifetime service to Grace. We want to rename a street after you. Not any street, Homer, but Main Street. It runs by your mama's grave over on the east side of town, right through Courthouse Square, and over to the west past your estate. We thought it was a proper way to show you the respect and love we all feel. What do you think about that?"

Homer was, for the first time Carl could remember, speechless. A quiet, peaceful moment ensued, and tears began to form—genuine tears from emotions that ran deep in Homer. But the world was not so quiet. Homer and Carl could hear the Agapovs in the Lincoln Town Car stretch limousine, jamming to a disco beat.

Homer bought the limo used. Complete with a ten-year-old, state-of-the-art sound system and interior flashing purple lights. Homer rode in the furthest back seat on most trips with an assortment of bourbons, orange juice, and emergency cranberry juice for when his bladder acted up. Vladimir drove, and Valentina sat behind the driver's seat, minding the nine kids scattered between her and Homer.

IT'S ABOUT THE LAND AND THE LEGACY

Each morning, the kids piled in, and the entourage proceeded to the Comprehensive School. All the grades were represented, including kindergarten for Sasha. After the kids exited, the three adults headed over to Grace Independent Grocery Store. Valentina liked to purchase produce daily, even though the manager changed the inventory weekly. While she shopped, Vladimir joined Homer in the back of the limo for an orange juice and discussed world history, politics, economics, or the fine points of gutting a pig. Vladimir was both worldly and practical at the same time. He would sometimes quote Pushkin. Or maybe Abraham Lincoln. Sometimes Popular Mechanics. But their conversations were always interesting.

Homer regained his composure and, for the first time, seemed at peace and was wistful. He realized that if the people of Grace were going to honor him this way, that he was in a place that loved him, and the deception that his brothers perpetrated on him maybe wasn't so important now and could be forgiven and forgotten. Maybe, he could just be proud that his family had provided the land for Courthouse Square.

"A street?" Homer asked.

"Yes. I will make the arrangements myself," Carl replied.

"Carl, I like that idea. Can we add Mama's name to it?"

Carl thought for a minute. He pondered whether to take it back to the town council and decided to make an executive decision.

"I don't see why not. Sure. How about Angelina and Homer Pitts Avenue"

"Wonderful. When can we do it?"

"May 1st," Carl responded.

"Lovely. May Day is a Russian holiday, you know. The Agapovs will be delighted."

Homer stood with a few tears dripping down his cheeks, and for once, he tried to hide them. Carl didn't press or ask since he knew how important this was to Homer. He just patted Homer on the back.

Carl waved to the Agapovs, who opened the limo windows to thrust out eleven hands rhythmically waving along with the pulsing beat of "YMCA."

"I said, young man, pick yourself off the ground/I said, young man, 'cause you're in a new town," they boisterously sang.

It was a favorite of the Agapovs and Homer's.

Later, Carl shared the news with Lula Bell. "I have always liked Homer," Lula Bell confided. "Thought he was pretty brave to go to New York City and chase his dreams. When he gave up everything to come back and take care of his dying mama, well, I just thought that was about as good as you could do. And you know he never mentions what he gave up. But he is also the kind of person who irritates you to death if you let him. It creates energy in him, I think. That's why I am usually irritable to him."

"I think we all just really love him," Carl added.

"Then let's just make sure we announce it at the celebration," Lula Bell offered.

Sunday, May 1st, the big day came, and the excitement attracted a crowd that filled the Courthouse Square. Scheduled for 2 p.m. on a warm, late spring afternoon, Carl presided over the assembly of honored guests on the podium. Everyone was there except Homer. With the sun shining brightly and things warming up, a stretch limo leisurely cruised down Main Street toward the gathering, with a police motorcycle escort no less. Grace didn't have a police motorcycle, but Sheriff Meeks borrowed an old one from a nearby police department for the afternoon. The motorcycle and limo pulled up to the podium where Main Street crossed the railroad track. The Agapov's piled out waving pom-poms, forming lines on either side of the sidewalk. Down the sidewalk, Vladimir unrolled a red carpet that Myrtle Hamby at the fabric store contributed. Valentina had painstakingly stitched the edges with gold tassel so it would look royal. The marching band assembled the twenty-five-member Grace High School and began playing "This Land is Your Land," mostly in tune. They had practiced.

Then out stepped Homer wearing a brilliant white tuxedo with tails, a top hat, and a baton to wave at the crowd. Cheers went up. He headed toward the courthouse, shaking as many hands as he could. Once assembled on the courthouse steps, Carl offered a few welcoming remarks. The Reverend Jackson gave the invocation mentioning Homer, love, and Grace in the same sentence. Sheriff Meeks celebrated Homer as a model non-violent protestor, and Lula Bell expressed the town's pride in Homer's service to the community's culture.

Then it was time for the unveiling.

Carl read the inscription under the street sign. "In honor of their cultural contributions to the town of Grace, Georgia, we rename Main Street as Angelina and Homer Pitts Avenue. With our admiration, love, and affection. The People of Grace."

More cheers went up.

Carl turned to Homer and offered him the microphone for a few words.

HOMER'S GRACE

As the drape came off, Homer could see the large, beautiful sign. Homer hesitated as he approached the microphone. He looked out over the excited, smiling crowd. A little boy yelled out, "We love you, Mr. Homer!" and the crowd roared with cheers and applause. Homer paused, then spoke with a joyous heart and grateful tears. "I love y'all too."

Afterward, a barbecue soiree at Homer's estate, a pretty expensive gift to the town, was a big hit. Pulled pork, potato salad, coleslaw, and white bread, and minty sweet tea. Homer put to rest his agitation over land. He felt loved and respect until, in the middle of the barbecue, Sheriff Meeks rode Homer's pet llama, Horatio, into the Olympic-sized pool!

CHAPTER 2

A LLAMA-INSPIRED FIASCO BEGINS

The following day, Homer slipped out the back door of his mansion and strolled out into his yard. His silk robe fell open to reveal his white tank top, plaid cotton pajama bottoms and untied hiking boots as he sipped a latte on the beautiful, fresh Monday morning. In the distance, beyond the hedge around the pool, he could see Horatio quietly eating grass in the pasture. Horatio looked happy and certainly no worse for the wear after a near-drowning the day before. Homer also thought about the hero of the afternoon—Mikhail. Diving into the pool, Mikhail acted quickly to save Horatio. Then Mikhail dove back in to save Sheriff Meeks. Carrying the inebriated and unresponsive sheriff in his arms like a sack of potatoes, Mikhail exited and laid the sheriff on a cushioned lounge by the pool. Mikhail thought he might have to give mouth-to-mouth resuscitation to the sheriff, but a geyser of pool water shot up from the sheriff as he regained consciousness. Coughing fits finally subsided, and Mikhail dried and cleaned the sheriff up a bit. When the ambulance came, the paramedics checked the sherriff's vital signs and performed a preliminary exam. Everything checked out okay. But in an abundance of caution, the ambulance crew insisted that it was their responsibility to take the sheriff to the hospital. Once he arrived at the hospital and the pain set in, the sheriff insisted that he needed to stay overnight. The doctors and nurses reluctantly agreed.

And also, on this beautiful Monday morning, a video of the previous day's event went viral on YouTube, with forty million views since it was posted late Sunday afternoon. Homer's home was now being broadcast on screens from Times Square to Red Square. The video captured Homer recounting the events at the celebration and giving a speech about Horatio while carrying his drink and directing emergency personnel. It repeatedly played worldwide in restaurants and electronics stores, schools and churches, barbershops, and beauty salons. And it played in the London boardroom of the international conglomerate, Swiss St. Clare, where a group of young associates had assembled for their usual Monday morning operations lunch meeting. On this particular Monday, a flabby, hairy, rotund young intern hijacked the session by providing a running commentary on the video as he played it over and over. The young man, Leopold St. Clare, was the third cousin, twice removed, of the firm's chairman and president, Count Armand St. Clare. Armand's great-great-aunt, Livia St. Clare Dawkins, had known Armand when he was young. Armand had always had a soft spot for Livia, his youngest great-great-aunt. So, at her request, Armand agreed to look after Leopold when she died since Leopold's parents and grandparents and great grandparents were, suffice it to say, eccentrically incapable. Leopold's boarding school in Scotland, trips worldwide, and an assortment of hobbies and pursuits were all financed by Armand. But Leopold was constitutionally unable

A LLAMA-INSPIRED FIASCO BEGINS

to hold down a real job. So, Armand had made space in London for Leopold to at least have somewhere to go each day.

Archibald DeSaliere, otherwise known as Archie, managed the London office of the Suisse St. Clare. Archie occupied a glass-walled office at the end of the floor where he could easily see the goings-on in the boardroom and scan the cubicles on the floor. Nothing escaped his keen, hawk-like gaze. He even had a microphone in each office that he could turn on from his desk. Mostly, he listened to the staff conversations but occasionally, he barked out a command—sort of like the voice of God from on high.

As he watched Leopold dance around, giggling and guffawing at the video, Archie focused his attention on the running headline at the bottom of the video. With each viewing, what captured his attention was the interview of a strange little man who, with bugged-out eyes and continuous delivery, informed the audience on the goings-on at what appeared to be his estate in rural Georgia. Archie recognized familiar features in the little man and the name Homer that seemed to be beyond coincidence. It took Archie a while to put it all together, but when he did, he had a strong desire to contact the good Count which he finally did. Urgently.

"Count St. Clare, good afternoon," Archie said.

"Archie, how are you, my good man? I am having a splendid afternoon by the shores of Lake Geneva in the fresh Swiss air. How are things in London?" The Count said, more talkative than usual.

"Foggy. Count, I have something that will interest you. A video has gone viral worldwide. It's very relevant to our many conversations about your past. And most important for the future I think.

Have your assistant get to the estate. Go on YouTube and search for these three words: Llama, Grace, Pool."

"Archie? You know I don't watch those things!" the Count replied with an air of disgust.

"Please, do it, Count. It's imperative and, what's more, quite humorous."

As the Count lounged on the patio of his four-story mansion on the shores of Lake Geneva, his young assistant came over with a book-sized iPad, the video queued up ready to play. Once the Count pressed play, a close-up came into view—a shrieking little man wearing a white Panama hat, open purple bath robe covering a yellow tank top, and green polka dot board shorts. An exciting and quite esthetically pleasing fashion collection, the Count thought. As the little man continued to shriek, the camera panned around to a llama ridden by a uniformed law officer galloping toward and then diving into an enormous swimming pool. Several other guests were seen, drinks in hand, laughing hysterically. The camera finally came back to the agitated little man, still shrieking but stopping intermittently to take sips from a now foaming champagne flute. The eighty-eight-year-old Count's eyes widened, and his mouth dropped open. Height, age, facial structure, and fashion sense seemed to fit someone the Count never knew existed.

"It's him!" the Count muttered.

"Yes, it's him," Archie said.

"Archie! It's him."

"Count, I know!"

"After more than fifty years, I know it's him!" the Count exclaimed

A LLAMA-INSPIRED FIASCO BEGINS

with growing ecstasy.

"Yes, Count. I do believe it could be him." Archie was more cautious.

"What do we do?' the Count asked.

"Well, I believe we have to investigate, quietly, and as soon as possible. We don't have much time. So, with your permission, I would like to dispatch Mr. Elliot."

"Discreetly," the Count whispered.

"Of course," Archie replied.

"Keep me informed. And what is my nitwit 3rd cousin up to?" the Count asked.

"Believe it or not, your third cousin, twice removed, found this video. He has been playing it nonstop for the last two hours for the firm's associates."

"I see. If only the idiot could turn that energy into something useful. Poor boy. I do wish he could get himself together so I could leave him something important. After all, he is my only living blood."

"Yes. Well, maybe this little video will lead us to an alternative for you."

"Right-O. Well, keep me informed," and the Count was gone.

Archie flipped to contacts on his cell phone and punched in Captain Monroe Elliot, Esq. Mr. Elliot still liked to go by his military rank of Captain from his days in the U.S. Marines. While in the service, Captain Elliot worked in intelligence, where he investigated and conducted surveillance on six continents. And although the Captain spoke seven languages and had black belts in jiujitsu, aikido, and taekwondo, he was also of average height and weight, with brown eyes, brown hair, no tattoos or scars, and he dressed conservatively. Most people wouldn't remember his presence at, for example, a party or church service. He was stealthy.

Captain Elliot left the military two decades earlier for law school and the FBI. For the past five years, he quietly made a fortune as the personal investigator for Archie and the Count on Swiss St. Clare official matters and matters of a more personal nature. There were two bank accounts. This investigation would be paid out of the personal account, even though it may very well have a significant, almost explosive, effect on the business. More than a billion dollars of equity in the company was at stake in this investigation—much more.

"Elliot here," answered the Captain.

"I am going to send you a link from YouTube," Archie said quickly. "I need you to conduct a deep background on the man identified in the video as Homer Pitts. This investigation is most urgent, and you must be discreet—very discreet. Only contact me on this cell phone for updates. Double your usual fee if you can get a complete workup in the next 72 hours."

"Got it. Visuals or just electronic?"

"Visual. Let's say that the fate of Swiss St. Clare rests in the balance. Call me with a preliminary report when you are in place for a visual. And you will need DNA."

"Oh! That's what this is. Understood. Talk soon." Captain Elliot hung up.

Homer walked the pasture and quietly approached Horatio. Towering over Homer, the white llama stood tall as Homer stroked his side with the usual affection he had shown over the last few years, even as the llama made Homer's little barbecue the day before a media sensation. When Homer decided he wanted a menagerie of animals that included some exotics, a friend suggested alpacas. "They have better, more lucrative fleece" was the advice. But Homer wanted a llama. Llamas had a longer face, a larger body, and Horatio was an excellent guard for Homer's other animals in the pasture. And llamas were excellent spitters.

Homer liked that Llamas were excellent spitters because he was an excellent spitter himself. The skill was acquired as a necessity in middle school when the other boys were trying out chewing tobacco. Homer didn't enjoy chewing tobacco, but he desperately wanted to fit in with a crowd of elitist, tough-boy wannabes who thought they were gangsters, albeit nerdy ones, and who felt they needed to chew tobacco to prove their manhood. Homer abhorred tobacco, even the thought of it, so he would stick a wad of gum in his cheek, keep his head down so no one could see the pink gum in his mouth, and spit too. But his spit was clear, not brown like the other boys. So, he embedded a little chocolate in the gum, and his spit turned brown. Then he was one of the boys. For a while, at least. When the ringleader of the little group, Johnny Longfellow, swallowed a wad of chewing tobacco after lunch and threw up his spaghetti and meatballs, the boys quit chewing tobacco. But Homer he kept spitting despite its loss in popularity—but without the chocolate. He perfected his spitting so that he could hit a miscreant from several feet away right in the eye and stop them dead in their tracks—sort of like the llamas. And alpacas, which Homer found out later, also spit. But he still liked his llama best.

While Homer was with Horatio, Mikhail took a morning jog through the forest on the estate. He liked the fresh air and the various animals: whitetail deer, foxes, rabbits, turkeys—sometimes even a coyote or bobcat. Mikhail wasn't a hunter. He usually had a 35mm camera with him, and he could sometimes snap a vivid, candid picture of what he saw. There were rumors that a black bear would wander onto the property occasionally, but Mikhail had not seen him. Then there were Homer's animals in the pasture near the house. The celebrity right now was Horatio. But there were also six goats, a peacock, two teacup pigs, and a Shetland pony. The last leg of Mikhail's jog came up through the pasture on his way back to the mansion. He finished at the work shed so he could put feed out for the exotic animals. All the animals rushed up to the shed when Mikhail came. Except for the little teacup pigs. Homer fed them by hand twice a day. They loved Homer and squealed delight when he came out to the pasture. Except now since they were napping over in some mud under a willow tree near the mountain side of the pasture. After feeding the animals, Mikhail usually went inside for Mama's breakfast. This morning, Mama waved him over to the table where Homer, Papa, and she were already eating as he headed in the back door. The other kids were still sleeping since it was the first day of the school kids' spring break.

Mikhail, now twenty, was very tall, athletic in build, and possessing exquisite, good looks that only excellent genetics and a robust lifestyle could provide. High school girls in Grace regularly came to play with his sisters to get a good look at Mikhail. Part of the society lady's reading club's attraction was that Mikhail served the teas to his many fawning middle-aged admirers. Not only was Mikhail pretty to look at, but he was wickedly smart as well. When the Agapovs arrived in the U.S., Mikhail already had his Russian secondary school certificate and was ready for university. He took the American GED and got a perfect score. And for the last two years since they arrived, Mikhail helped Papa with the house and estate, which Mikhail enjoyed. He knew that the adults wanted him to go to a prestigious American university. Still, he was ambivalent about that direction, although he had not expressed the ambivalence or any alternatives to his parents or Mister Homer. But that was about to change.

"Mikhail, our hero!" Homer cheered. "You saved the llama, the Sheriff, and our celebration yesterday!"

"Thank you, Mister Homer. I am simply happy I could help." His Russian accent was still strong. Small talk and a recanting of the past afternoon's humorous events followed, eventually leading to the day's primary topic of discussion.

"Mikhail. It is time for you to leave," Papa said bluntly with a sad face. Mikhail appeared puzzled and a little scared.

"What do you mean, Papa?" Mikhail asked.

"You need to go to university," Mama said as she entered the conversation with visible trepidation. Mama loved having her oldest boy at home, but she also knew he had to have his own life at some point.

"What?" Mikhail was more confused.

"You are a brilliant boy, Mikhail. You scored a perfect score on the GED test. And here are your college admissions scores." Homer slid an envelope across the table as he talked. Homer sneaked a peek at the scores and knew what Mikhail's reaction would be when he opened the envelope and scanned the results. In anticipation, a slight smile came over Homer's face. Mikhail smiled as he studied the report.

"So, how did you do?" Papa asked carefully.

"Perfect score," Mikhail responded casually.

"Okay. Then it's university time, Mikhail. We need to get you to a top-notch university," Homer said triumphantly.

"I don't care about the university. I want to be a butler."

Papa, Mama, and Homer all looked at Mikhail with wide eyes and gaping mouths. A lengthy, dead silence ensued.

"Butler?" Papa said slowly and with uncertainty.

"A butler." Homer defined the term for the Agapovs. "The man of the house. Defined as the head male servant who coordinates guests and greetings, meals, drinks, and anything else that needs doing. Mikhail, why do you want to be a butler?"

"Butlers are cool," he exclaimed. "Alfred Pennyworth, Reginal Jeeves, Benson DuBois or Charles Carson. They can handle any situation, and they are the ones who know what is going on in the mansions and estates where they work. I would like to be like that."

"Well, I can see you have been watching quite a bit of TV reruns and superhero movies," Homer quipped.

"And top butlers make over a hundred thousand dollars per year, have room and board paid, a car provided, and four weeks of vacation," Mikhail added.

"Well, okay. Have you given any thought as to where you would like to be a butler?" Homer followed up.

"Here, Mister Homer. Here at the estate."

"But you would need to be trained. Or go to school, preferably."

"London School of Butlers," Mikhail answered.

"What? A school for butlers?" Mama said.

"Yes. Most prestigious in the world, and I will receive a certificate

A LLAMA-INSPIRED FIASCO BEGINS

from the Queen."

"My, oh, my. Have you been researching this?" Homer added.

"Yes, I have. I have considered university, but that doesn't interest me. I am a practical person. I see the need for coordination here at the estate, and I can do that very well. But, I agree, I need training. And I believe I am smart and talented enough to do well at the best school for butlers in the world." Mikhail surprised everyone and seemed to be serious and intent on his path. It was clear he loved the estate as much as Homer. Mikhail loved nature, the mansion, and serving. Butlership would be the best way to have it all, he figured. Mama began to cry tears of joy that her oldest boy would continue to live there. But she immediately saw the problem. She also wanted grandchildren, and no self-respecting woman good enough for her Mikhail would come live in the mansion. There were only five bedrooms, and everyone knew that Homer insisted on at least one spare bedroom for guests. A home for her boy would have to be addressed.

While Valentina considered how they would deal with the housing situation, across town, Mayor Carl also considered an issue he had to address. The town council just finished an emergency meeting on the already hot and increasingly muggy Monday morning to discuss the disgraceful way Grace's sheriff had become the subject of a globally viral video showing him drunk and riding a llama into a pool. The discussion by the council was short but intense. The decision was that Sheriff Meeks would have to retire, and a new sheriff would be recruited immediately. In the interim, Deputy Jessup would be the acting Sheriff. Carl got the task of going to the hospital to break the news to Sheriff Meeks.

CHAPTER 3

THE BLUE MUSTANG

"Lula Bell, I have to go out to the hospital to deliver some bad news," Carl said.

"Did somebody die?" Lula Bell yelled out as she rolled dough in the kitchen for a pie.

"Well, I don't think I would be going out to the hospital to tell them somebody died, dear. Usually, the other way around. So no, I don't have to do that."

"Oh. Well, somebody going to jail?" Lula Bell asked as she clicked down her mental list.

"Again, no."

"Somebody losing their home? Their land?"

"Nope."

"Okay then, well, you must be firing someone. Who are you firing?"

"Sheriff Meeks."

"Good. After that fiasco yesterday at Homer's party, it serves him right. A man ought to know better than to act like that kind of fool!"

Carl smiled as he thought about Lula Bell's assessment, and he hoped he never crossed her by doing something stupid like the sheriff.

After fifty years of marriage, he was sure that Lula Bell would say that any punishment Carl got was "well-deserved." He gave her a peck on the cheek and galloped out to the car, his pride and joy; a blue 1971 Ford Mustang Boss 351 that he finally pulled out of its mausoleum. The beauty roared to life instantly as if it had just rolled off the assembly line. He eased off the clutch and pulled out of the garage. The rumbling pristine car was a sight to behold.

For the better part of almost fifty years, the Mustang sat out back in a hermetically sealed one-car garage. His father bought it for him in 1972 but never gave it to him. Dad kept saying Carl needed to grow up some more before he would get the car. Carl joined the Navy to convince his Dad that he was brave enough to handle the 351. But then Dad had a heart attack and died while Carl was away in the service. Carl came home on emergency family leave with a heavy heart and guilt that he had not lived up to his father's expectations soon enough. After the funeral, Carl locked up the garage with a chain and padlock. It stayed like that for the next 45 years until a few weeks earlier. Carl got to thinking that it was disrespectful for the vehicle to sit all alone decade after decade in that one-car garage. He couldn't undo his time with his father, nor would he want to. And his dad was not coming back. But he figured he could honor his father's dreams for Carl by taking the 351 out and driving it.

As Carl headed out toward the four-lane highway in the 351 toward the hospital, he was at peace—finally driving the last thing his daddy was going to give him—forty-five years after the fact. And once Carl got a little breathing room, he gunned the 351 to see how fast she could go. The rumble from the pulsing engine was invigorating for Carl. The wind passing by his open window felt like a jet exhaust as he hit 90 miles per hour, rounding a curve about ten miles from the hospital. It was at just that moment that he saw the flashing blue light in his rearview mirror. He didn't recognize the car behind him. So it wasn't someone from the Grace Sheriff's office. He slowed down and pulled up onto the curb. Reaching into the glove compartment, he had to strain to get to his registration. He grunted pretty loudly.

"Hold it right there. Don't you move!" a woman's voice called out. The voice was feminine, he thought, but with manly overtones. He waited, frozen in an uncomfortable stretching position. And waited. And waited. His arm was cramping, so he called out to the officer to see if he could sit up. But no answer came back. Did the lady cop leave? He wasn't sure. Now he had a real dilemma. Dare he sit up only to have his head blown off by a trigger-happy cop? Or should he stay in his current position until he passes out? The only thing he could rationally do was call out again, as loud as he could.

"Can I sit up!!!" Carl yelled.

"Sir, why are you yelling?" the lady cop was right at the car window, so close that he could feel her breath on his back. Why didn't she answer the first time, he thought?

"Ma'am, may I sit up, please?" he asked sheepishly.

"Yes, sir. Need to see driver's license and registration."

Carl sat up and relieved the muscle spasm that wrenched his back out of alignment. He brought the registration with him as he sat up and then reached for his wallet to get his license, all before looking at the officer.

Carl almost wet himself when he did finally gaze at the officer. Very tall. Scary tall. Her hair was short and blonde—straight with no highlights or embellishments of any kind. She wore reflective aviator-style sunglasses and a ball cap with "U.S. Special Forces" in gold letters on the brim. Her face was chiseled like Mount Rushmore. Her shoulders broad, her arms muscular. His wife was large but no longer the only Amazonian warrior princess in Grace. But who was this officer?

"Here you go, Officer," Carl said as he forked over the license and registration. "Why didn't you answer the first time I called out?"

"Carl Longfellow. Aren't you the Mayor of Grace?" the officer exclaimed while ignoring his question. She seemed to be selective in her responses.

"Why yes, how did you know?" Carl said with a smile.

"Billboard," she replied. Carl forgot that his pleasant face was on billboards coming in and out of Grace. It was part of a campaign to help visitors feel at home. There was one about a hundred yards up the road.

"Yes, part of our campaign. And Officer . . ." he tried to see her name, but the badge obscured her nametag. All he could make out was "–insky." It sounded Slavic, maybe Polish, he thought. "Are you new here in Grace?"

"I am not in Grace, sir. I was just passing through. Do you realize that I clocked you at 102 miles per hour in a 55 mile per hour zone?" she asked. Carl looked at her and thought it best not to contest the speed. And if she wasn't in Grace, why was she pulling him over here, in Grace?

"No, ma'am, I didn't realize I was going that fast," Carl said sheepishly. "Well, where are you, a law officer, if I may ask?"

"I work for the State Bureau, sir." The State Bureau investigated murders and terrorist attacks. Why was she pulling him over?

"So, sugar, you think I am a terrorist?" Carl blurted out with a smile, trying to be congenial, he thought. But he knew when he saw her face that the "sugar" and the question were mistakes—big uns.

"So, are you saying you are a terrorist? Out of the car now and spread 'em." She stepped back from the car in a swift, fluid movement and pulled open the door, all with her trusty 9mm Glock pistol drawn and ready to fire. Carl thought that this was a classic escalating situation. What came next would be even more thrilling.

"Officer, I am obeying your commands," Carl said as he slowly exited, spread his legs wide, and leaned against the car. "I want you to know that I am not a terrorist. I am the Mayor of Grace, Georgia." As he was exiting, Carl saw his life flash before his eyes. Childhood, teenage years, marriage, children, real estate, golf.

"Got it, sir. I see that you are now trying to throw your weight around. Well, I am going to have to charge you twice then, but frankly, I don't have a ticket book, so we will have to call your sheriff."

"Sheriff Meeks? He is critically ill in the hospital. That's where I was going," Carl said, exaggerating the sheriff's condition.

"Ill. What happened to him?" The officer seemed to relax a little bit.

"Near drowning," Carl replied.

"In the line of duty?" she asked.

"You could say that." Carl was milking this to try to get out of the tickets.

"Well, why didn't you say that in the beginning? Get in your car and follow me."

Officer "-insky" got in her cruiser, put on the blue light and siren, and proceeded to disco drive—a term Carl made up when he was young. Carl came of age in the 1970s during disco. The tempo in disco is 120 beats per minute. It's pretty fast, but back then, Carl got the hang of it the more he went to dances courting a younger Lula Bell. And he started driving a hot rod, so he came up with a magical synthesis of speed in two dimensions: music and cars. And disco driving was born on the backroads of north Georgia. And reborn as Carl and the law officer took off for the hospital.

Out they went at 120 miles per hour. Carl started humming his favorite disco song—Gloria Gaynor's "I Will Survive." Technically, the beat for that hit was 116 beats per minute. But it was close enough, and the words were particularly appropriate as they raced down the four-lane, passing log trucks and the Memories van from the Grace Nursing Home. Carl hadn't had so much exhilarating fun since he was nineteen. Whoever this lady agent was, she could drive better than any law officer Carl had met. They arrived at the hospital entrance in seven minutes. The agent cleared the way with a dramatic flourish, entering the lobby with her hands up. The excitement in the hospital would soon surpass the excitement of the drive there.

CHAPTER 4

A TERRORIST ATTACK

"Let's clear the way here for the Mayor, folks. Got an emergency underway," the officer said with authority. Elmer Longfellow, Carl's cousin, was a patient in the hospital who just happened to be in the lobby with his wife, Maureen, walking around as the doctor had ordered. He was recovering from a bout of pneumonia. The couple walked through the hospital corridors to get some exercise and ended up in the lobby just as the commotion occurred.

"Carl, what's going on?" Elmer called out as Carl rushed by. Carl didn't have time to think, much less answer. Elmer noticed that the rather tall woman with Carl had a cap that read "U.S. Special Forces" and big yellow letters on the back of her bulletproof vest that read "State Bureau."

"Maureen, that woman looks like she is one of them terrorist hunters, doesn't she?" Elmer asked.

"Elmer, I believe you are right. Maybe we have a terrorist attack?" Maureen responded.

"Better call Myrtle Hanby down at the fabric store. She will know. Carl looked like he was busy," Elmer suggested.

"Or terrified. Poor Lula Bell. I should go over there and comfort her," Maureen replied.

"Well, get me back to the room. Maybe I can find out from the nurses what's going on and call you later," Elmer said.

"Okay. Let's go." Maureen replied.

The officer and the Mayor exited the elevator on the second floor of the two-floor hospital. With only fifty beds and a two-stretcher emergency room, Grace Comprehensive Hospital was light on the comprehensiveness. It was mostly for people near the end and didn't want to leave town or people who weren't sick enough to be in the hospital but needed a rest or a place to hide. The latter was the category into which Sheriff Meeks fit.

"Sheriff, I want you to meet Officer . . . ." Carl hesitated. He still couldn't read her nameplate. The badge and the nameplate were mashed together, and the only part of her name that was visible was still "—-insky." But she spoke up.

"Good morning, Sheriff. I am Officer Brunhilde Inksy." The officer said it so fast that Carl still wasn't sure what her name was. Dinsky? Insky? Or was she saying her full name, Brunhildinsky? It wasn't a name with which he was familiar, anyway. And he wasn't in the disposition to ask right now. His thoughts went back to the sheriff.

"How are you doing?"

"Oh, Carl. I am in such pain. My neck is crooked, and my back is out. Broken fibula. Liver tests all whacked out. And the worst thing is my headache."

"Sirs, I am going to step out in the hallway while you discuss this confidential patient information. Excuse me." The officer exited

A TERRORIST ATTACK

before either man could say anything more.

"Carl, that's the tallest, scariest looking woman I have ever seen."

"She gave me a police escort to the hospital. I am in the Mustang and got her wide open! She can drive, man. She can drive!"

"You mean the officer or the Mustang?"

"Both. By the way, Sheriff, do you know her?"

"Nope. It looks like she is from the State Bureau. Those guys don't talk to us, local yokels."

"Oh. Well, anyway, it sounds like you are in pretty rough shape." Carl was hoping that this might be a moment that he could gently introduce the idea of retirement. He was wrong.

"I hurt, but they are letting me go home in about an hour. Should be back to the office tomorrow."

"I see. Well, have you thought about the video and how you are going to explain that to your officers?"

"What video?"

Carl looked at Sheriff Meeks for a long, torturous moment. Carl realized that this poor man who valued his privacy and anonymity had no idea that he was the star of the most viewed video currently on YouTube. In the world. Even though Carl thought using the humiliation of the moment to end the sheriff's career was both cruel and cowardly, he still believed that it was the right thing to do.

"Sheriff, let me show you something." Carl pulled out his iPhone and started the video. He turned the sound up to almost full for effect. Carl was sure that the footage would embarrass the sheriff and lead to introspection and humiliation. But he felt he had to do it anyway.

"Cool! A celebrity? I am world famous, Carl!" the sheriff responded.

The reaction mystified Carl. He expected tears, pleas for forgiveness, and, most likely, something akin to a nervous breakdown. Instead, the sheriff seemed to believe he had received a gift.

"My grandkids will love it! Papaw is a celebrity! Right here in little ole Grace, Georgia." He watched it again and again. Five times in total, without so much as expressing a moment of concern or regret. He seemed to think that there was a future in video for him.

"Carl, I wonder if I should go back out there to Homer's and do another video with the llama. Maybe in the pasture doing some trick riding?"

"Trick riding? What in the Lord's name are you talking about, Sheriff? You don't realize that you look foolish and made the town look foolish?" Carl was a little annoyed now, but he didn't go so far as to say to the sheriff that the town council fired him that morning. Not yet, at least.

"Carl, you need to get up with the times. Ever heard the phrase, "there's no such thing as bad publicity"?" Sheriff Meeks wasn't joking.

Carl looked at the sheriff in shock. Carl was diplomatic by nature, but enough was enough.

"Sheriff Meeks, I am afraid the town council sees it differently. We met this morning, reviewed the video, and reached a unanimous decision to terminate your employment as sheriff, effective today."

"What?" Sheriff Meeks suddenly appeared helpless and confused. Carl had some wiggle room to offer a two-week notice, continued benefits, and retirement pension. But he needed to get the sheriff's attention first, which he now had. But maybe he went a little overboard. The now trembling sheriff looked at Carl with widened eyes,

A TERRORIST ATTACK

silent. Finally, words leaked out of his quivering lips.

"Oh no," and with those two words, the trembling sheriff passed out.

After a few seconds of stillness, a nurse ran into the room with a big red cart. "He is fibrillating."

Carl wasn't sure what she meant, but he knew it couldn't be good. Carl exited the room to the hallway. The sheriff's room was at the end of a half-filled hall. A pair of wooden doors with windows bisected the hallway about halfway. Insky was standing in front of the doors restricting movement to the area where the sheriff was located. No one knew why except her. Maybe she thought she was providing security or something. Anyway, she did have enough presence of mind to allow the nurses running down the hall toward the sheriff's room to pass unimpeded. But no one else, including the sheriff's sister, Mildred, promptly passed out and hit the floor. Mildred had been checking in on the sheriff since his wife died a couple of years back and his grown children had moved away. Mildred always had a weak constitution, and this time she thought that her brother must be dead but that no one was telling her.

Carl stood awkwardly in the hallway. The visitors held up by Insky could see him and started questioning why the mayor was back there by the sheriff's room during an emergency.

Terrorists. The word had already traveled from Maureen Longfellow to Lula Bell and then Myrtle Hanby at the fabric store. From these two lovely ladies, the story made it to the book club ladies and Valentina. And Valentina passed it on to Homer.

"Mister Homer, Mister Homer!" Valentina ran at full speed for a large rotund lady to find Homer. He was still out in the pasture, enjoying the late spring smell of American wisteria blooms that grew on some of the trees nearby. He brought a book with him: Epictetus, the Stoic Philosopher.

"Yes, Valentina. What is it?"

"Mister Homer, we have a terrorist attack!" she breathlessly spouted as she stopped to catch her breath.

"A terrorist attack," Homer pondered. Could he apply Epictetus in this situation? he wondered. An attack could be neither good nor bad, but could it depend on how Homer used it? Or could he remain indifferent to it and pursue virtue instead?

"Valentina, do you mean the United States has a terrorist attack? Maybe in New York?"

"No, Mister Homer. It's here in Grace. At the hospital."

"At the hospital?" Homer thought deeply. He could not figure out how a terrorist would have an interest in the Grace Comprehensive Hospital. At that moment, his cell phone rang.

"Homer, I have heard that a terrorist attack has occurred at the hospital. And my Carl is out there right now!" Lula Bell anxiously told Homer.

"Lula Bell, calm down. What terrorist attack? Why are there terrorists in Grace?"

"Well, all I know is that Maureen saw Carl and an agent from the U.S. Special Forces enter the hospital, and now he is quarantined with the sheriff."

"Quarantined?"

"Yes. And I think the sheriff died. I heard that he was fibrillating!"

Sheriff Meeks fainted due to something called the vasovagal reflex.

A TERRORIST ATTACK

Too much stress and the vagus nerve that runs through your neck slows the heart rate down until you pass out. Not always or in everyone, but Sheriff Meeks was sensitive to the change. When the call to the nurse's station came that the sheriff had passed out, a new nurse, Connie Marlboro, looked at the cardiac monitor and saw a wiggling, fast-paced line. She thought that was fibrillating. Connie grabbed the crash cart and hit the code 99 button, all in the same movement. She was fast and beat everyone to the room by a full ten seconds. She started chest compressions on the sheriff until a few seconds later when the sheriff screamed out in agony—just as the other nurses entered the room. Apparently, Connie's compressions were so forceful with her total weight put into them that she cracked three of the Sheriffs' ribs—snap, crackle, pop. Connie was a relatively short but large woman, sort of like a bowling ball. A two-hundred-pound bowling ball bouncing up and down on Meeks' chest at 100 beats per minute. The screams that the sheriff let out could be described as "bloodcurdling." The visitors with cell phones being held at bay by Inksy shared recordings of the terror with their friends on Instagram and Twitter.

"The poor sheriff is screaming out in agony. It must be a biological weapon. Maybe Ebola." Maureen gave a firsthand account over the phone to Lula Bell. She never left the hospital after she took Elmer back to his room. There hadn't been this much excitement in Grace in a long time. They finished up their conversation, and Lula Bell returned Homer's call. By the time the call came in on Homer's cell, he was dressed in his summer traveling suit and headed to the hospital in the limo, with Vladimir driving and Mikhail along to learn something that might come in handy as a butler. And little

Ludmilla, who wanted to be an infectious disease doctor someday, couldn't miss her opportunity to see a biological terrorist attack. She was only eleven now but already prepped and ready with her scuba mask, air pipe, bleach spray, and her hazmat suit she got at the Halloween costume store.

Meanwhile, at the hospital, two doctors arrived on the scene in the sheriff's room. Dr. Hippo, whose real name was Dr. Adebayo, was a Nigerian-born family physician in Grace. Dr. Youssef was an Egyptian-born internist who joined Dr. Hippo a year later. Both men did their residencies in Atlanta then took advantage of the underserved primary care placements that sped their way to green cards and citizenship. Both men had been through much more than anyone knew or could appreciate. Yet, they were almost childlike in their optimism and grace. The town was a perfect home for them and their families.

Dr. Hippo was a huge man, six foot five inches tall and over 300 pounds, with a massive smile, a glistening bald head, and shiny white teeth. He loved to swim—in pools, lakes, or the ocean. He would dive under and emerge with just half his head peeking out of the water. Enough for his eyes and nose to be above the water. But every so often, he would jump up out of the water, surprising kids, and adults alike, like the hippos in the rivers of his youth in Nigeria. He did his little routine with all the kids at the pool in town. His kids, the other black kids, the white kids, the Hispanic kids. Everyone. All the kids giggled and jumped and splashed him. And eventually, the adult parents came around too. Dr. Hippo was fun to be around and a gracious and forgiving man.

Dr. Youssef was of small stature, lean and wiry. Dignified, quick,

A TERRORIST ATTACK

and efficient in his movements, he was also quiet, reflective, and brilliant. His eyes twinkled when he talked, with a rapid staccato type of speech and his voice was soft and low-pitched. The two men were quite a contrast but were professional colleagues in practice and the best of friends.

The pair of doctors assessed the medical situation in the room. Dr. Hippo spoke first. "This man does not have Ebola. I have seen Ebola. I have treated Ebola. Some of my family died of Ebola. This man does not have Ebola!" Then Dr. Youseff spoke. "I agree with my friend and colleague. This man has broken ribs. He does not have Ebola."

"Nurses, I would like to see an EKG," Dr. Hippo said. He would address the cardiac problem. Meeks had an EKG while he continued to sob with pain. Dr. Hippo looked at the rhythm on the machine as the EKG was running.

"This man does not have cardiac fibrillation. He has sinus tachycardia probably because he is in so much pain," Dr. Hippo pronounced.

"I agree with my esteemed colleague and great friend. Again, his judgment is impeccable. This man has sinus tachycardia, probably from the frightful pain of potentially broken ribs," Dr. Youssef added.

Dr. Hippo gave the nurse an order for a sedative and pain medicine, and he and Dr. Youseff, sensing their jobs were done, exited the room. They headed down the back stairwell to avoid the crowd in the hall near the elevators. They arrived and left the room without running into Betty Gilroy, the director of nursing. And the nurses in the room, especially Connie, really did think Meeks had been fibrillating.

While the town's sheriff was fibrillating and terrorists lurking, Deputy Seymour Jessup flipped through pictures online as he sat sipping a latte at the Grace Sheriffs Office. He wasn't supposed to be surfing the web looking at the images at work, but he couldn't control himself. It was an obsession bordering on a disorder—picture after picture and drooling as he went.

It wasn't porn, but Hot Wheels. Jessup was an avid collector looking for a particular collectible Hot Wheels car—the Number 271 Funny Car. The rarest collectible Hot Wheels car around, and with only six left in the world, finding one would be worth several thousand dollars. So, Jessup searched online every day. Hot Wheels were his driving passion, and his job as a deputy sheriff in a town with truly little crime allowed him to surf the web most of the day looking for his dream car. But on this Monday, he was thrust into a real-life emergency, sort of.

"Deputy Sheriff Jessup, have you heard anything yet about the terrorists?" The call was from retired Major A.B. Lowman, the town's historian.

"Terrorists?" Jessup asked.

"A couple of ladies called me about a terrorist attack at the hospital. But you haven't heard anything or gotten any calls?"

"Nope," Jessup responded.

"Worse than I thought," Major Lowman said.

"What do you mean?"

"If the attack is ongoing and you aren't aware, then it is an insurgency operation—many examples in history. By the time the National Guard gets here, it will be too late. Where's the sheriff?" Major Lowman was increasingly concerned.

"Still at the hospital, I believe. He was admitted last night."

A TERRORIST ATTACK

"Makes more sense now. Yes, chop off the head of the snake, and the body may writhe and curl, but it is essentially dead." Lowman could see the terrorist strategy more clearly now. Whatever took the sheriff to the hospital last night played into the hands of the terrorist masterminds. If the man in charge was already in the hospital when the attack started, the terrorists could take out the leader right away.

Major Lowman was a military man, retired to Grace from the U.S. Marines. He still had a crew cut and wore khaki pants with a short-sleeved khaki shirt as his uniform of the day, along with black combat boots. Major Lowman taught history at the Comprehensive School, was unmarried, and split his free time between Civil War reenactments, World War II model building with realistic dioramas, and the shooting range. He had prepared his entire life for the defense of America, and if needed, he would take things into his own hands. But he also needed to rouse and direct the troops.

"Deputy, my advice to you is to get out there to the hospital and set up roadblocks to contain the attack. And you need to call in all your off-duty officers immediately. You may be our only uniformed service to nip this attack in the bud. I will prepare to Counterattack from the forest near the hospital. It's only half a mile from my house, and if I double-time it, I can be in position within the hour. Let's get to work and Semper Fi, my good man, Semper Fi." And with that Major Lowman hung up. Deputy Jessup was perplexed. An attack at the Grace Comprehensive Hospital? It seemed like someone official would have let him know by now that there was an attack going on, especially if it required Jessup to bring in the off-duty deputy, Arnie Morris. Arnie had taken his family to Disney World this week since it was spring break. Deputy Jessup wasn't sure he had Morris' cell phone number or an email address or any way to contact Morris. For Deputy Sheriff Jessup, things were moving a little too fast. As he thought a few more moments, Jessup decided he needed to finish his Hot Wheels search for the day, and then he would head over to the hospital.

The director of nursing, Betty Gilroy, arrived on the second floor trying to find out what was going on. She came up from the first floor, where she saw that the lobby was full of extended family members and friends of the sheriff. Grace's first bioterrorism casualty, they said to her, needed their support in this difficult time. As did Mayor Carl, who was in quarantine apparently, with the sheriff. And thank goodness that the Special Forces lady was here to provide security and updates. The AM radio station sent their news director out to the hospital to interview the Special Forces lady. She only responded, "No comment at this time," to his rapid-fire, incessant questions. The news reporter said a "no comment" confirmed that a secret attack must be underway. Otherwise, the lady agent would have said there was no attack, wouldn't she?

CHAPTER 5

HOMER RESTORES ORDER—SORT OF

Homer and his entourage entered the hospital chaos while leaving the limo parked at the hospital entrance with emergency lights still blinking. As he entered the lobby, the townsfolk turned and clapped, with the goodwill of the previous day's celebration still fresh in their minds. Homer smiled and nodded as any visiting dignitary would. Heading to the elevators, Homer shook some hands and asked if anyone knew what was going on.

"Oh, Homer, it's so good you are here. You are pretty levelheaded. We just heard that the sheriff is dying, Carl is quarantine, and Mildred Meeks was injured! Unconscious, we think." The staccato report from Myrtle Hanby was a little hard for Homer to digest. Myrtle had closed the fabric store and headed straight out to the hospital to show her support.

"They think it's Ebola," she added.

Homer looked at Myrtle and the rest of the folks in the lobby. He had to admit that something didn't quite add up. Terrorist attack, a fibrillating sheriff, quarantined mayor, and now Ebola? He would have to gather some additional information to understand what was at the heart of it all.

"Well, I am here now, and I will get to the bottom of this. Be strong, my fellow people of Grace!" The thought crossed Homer's mind that since both the sheriff and mayor were incapacitated, he may have to step in, temporarily, to take charge of Grace. Especially with an impending war or epidemic or both. But he remembered the grief Alexander Haig got for stepping up too early when Reagan was shot. So, he kept the thought to himself.

Homer pushed through the crowd to the elevators along with Vladimir, Mikhail, and Ludmilla. He waved dramatically to the crowd as he boarded the elevator, and Ludmilla smiled. She was going to get to see her first case of Ebola, and she was only eleven.

"Homer is risking his life and taking charge for us! Our Churchill!" Myrtle cried out as she wiped her tears away with a swatch of daisy-covered cotton fabric just arrived at the fabric store for spring. The folks in the lobby cheered and clapped.

The crowd on the second floor thinned out a bit like the director of nursing began to restore order. A nurse at the hospital for thirty years, Betty Gilroy had never managed a terrorist attack. She needed to see the terrorist victim up close, so she tried to get past Insky at the double doors. She tried her authority first.

"I am Betty Gilroy, the director of nursing here, and I need to get back there to find out what's going on."

"Ma'am, are you needed to render care?" the agent asked.

"I don't know because I don't know what's going on, but . . . ." Betty tried to respond.

"Then the protocol for this situation is to restrict unnecessary movement, and since you don't know if you are needed, I will have to

HOMER RESTORES ORDER—SORT OF

▲

stop you here."

"Well, I understand, but I need to find out what's going on."

"I appreciate that, ma'am, but I need to ensure that the perimeter is secure. Can you show me some ID?"

Betty suddenly realized she had left her ID on her desk. An inconvenience, but she would be back in a couple of minutes.

"Okay, it's in my office, let me go fetch it," Betty responded.

"Not so quick, ma'am. We might have a bioterrorist attack here, so you need to stay on this floor—at least for now," Insky informed Betty.

"What? Are you nuts? A bioterrorist attack? Where?" Betty irately questioned.

"Behind these closed doors, I am told that the sheriff is dying a slow, cruel death. The mayor is back there with him now as well as the cardiac resuscitation team."

"Carl is back there? Sheriff Meeks just has a broken fibula. I thought he already went home." Betty said.

"Ma'am, I don't have complete information, but the sheriff was fibrillating a while ago. The team brought him back from the brink, but we kept hearing bloodcurdling screams from back there. We learned in my bioterror class that might indicate Ebola."

"Listen, honey. You need to get out my freakin' way so I can straighten this out!" the nursing director barked. Insky reassessed her position and decided to let Betty go back.

"Okay, director, head on back." Insky eased the door open slightly to allow the feisty, bantam-sized nursing director back into the hallway. Insky put her baton through the two opposing door handles and effectively locked everyone inside when the door shut. Insky now had regained operational control of the situation.

Sheriff Meeks calmed down to a quivering whimper as Connie examined his chest to see if there was anything more serious than the broken ribs. He squealed with each press but was beginning to appreciate the thoroughness of his savior and rib-breaker, Connie. As this exam was going on, Betty burst in and began to interrogate everyone in the room.

"What is going on here? Sheriff, why are you whimpering?"

"Oh, I ain't the sheriff no more!" He let out another run of loud sobbing.

Betty was unaware that Carl fired Meeks. She stood in the middle of the room with her hands on her hips, sternly quiet with a puzzled look on her face. At this point, Carl walked in. A few minutes before, while Betty had been allowed to come back by Insky, Carl had slipped into one of the many vacant hospital rooms nearby to use the toilet. When Carl entered Meeks' room again, Betty whipped around to ask him to explain but not before Meeks let out another blood-curdling scream at the sight of Carl. Carl looked at the sheriff with a mixture of pity and barely suppressible laughter. When the sheriff let out yet another squeal, Carl lost it and began to giggle. Betty, picking up that something was awry, took Carl aside.

"Carl, what's going on here?" Betty whispered.

"Betty, it's a bit complicated. As you know, the sheriff had a majorly embarrassing escapade out at Homer's place yesterday, along with a relatively minor medical problem. Well, the town council thought that he should resign. He didn't get it, so I fired him this morning. He overreacted and, well, one thing led to another, and we are where we are.

HOMER RESTORES ORDER—SORT OF

"Which is where, Carl?"

"A major fiasco, Betty."

"Who is the blonde giant out there obstructing the hallway?'

"I was driving a little too fast on the way over here this morning, and she pulled me over. Again, one thing led to another, and she ended up coming to the hospital with me. She is just trying to help with the crowd out there, I think."

"Carl, she is scaring people half to death! Send her away right now."

"Well, Betty, she doesn't work for us. She works at the State Bureau."

"Carl, are you on something? Drugs? Narcotics? What? This is the most hair-brained fiasco I have ever heard. Now go out there and tell her to go back to Atlanta, I guess, and let us get things calmed down. Now!" Betty was Lula Bell's second cousin. There were some similarities in their approaches to Carl.

Carl bowed his head like a puppy dog and walked back out into the hallway and up to the doors, which wouldn't open. He knocked on the window in the door to get Insky's attention. She turned and smiled at Carl, then held up a sign.

"Waiting for the Hazmat team from Atlanta. I called them, and they should be here in two hours. Until then, no entries or exits. FBI will be taking over the investigation since this may be a domestic attack."

Carl's stomach flipped. He felt a sense of disorientation and nausea and went back to the sheriff's hospital room to find a chair to sit in before he passed out like Meeks. Betty looked at Carl and surmised that the blonde giant refused to let him out. Well, Betty knew about the back stairwell, so she huffed out of the room, turned left, and went into the housekeeping room, then hung another left to go down the stairwell. Once Betty was on the first floor, she headed to her office. She had just missed Homer and his entourage, who were getting off the elevator on the second floor. Once Betty was back in her office, she wasn't exactly sure what she could do. Calming down might be an excellent place to start.

Homer exited the elevator. He brought along a walking cane even though he didn't need it to walk, but he thought it was classy along with his white Panama hat and his summer traveling suit. All white, with a green button-down shirt and yellow bow tie. And a yellow silk handkerchief for his coat pocket. He led a growing entourage down the hall to the double doors and Officer Insky.

"Good day, officer. I am Homer Pitts," Homer started. The officer seemed distracted.

"Yes, sir. Sorry, this wing is sealed off right now."

"Officer, may I inquire as to why that might be?"

"You may inquire, but I cannot disclose any information to the public at this point."

"Officer, that may be true, but I would like to remind you that failure to heed the request of an officer of the court can lead to criminal prosecution. So, I will ask again, what is going on here?" Homer chose his words expertly. He never said he was an officer of the court, only that failure to disclose would lead to prosecution. And he didn't specify what the prosecution would be for.

Insky yielded, sensing that Homer was someone important. She remembered seeing his name on the main street sign in town just that morning.

"In that case, sir, the sheriff is hospitalized in critical condition,

HOMER RESTORES ORDER—SORT OF

I believe, fibrillating and screaming from the pain of his Ebola. The mayor is back there with him, along with doctors, nurses, and the director of nursing. We believe it may be a bioterrorist attack."

Homer nodded his head, indicating that he was up to speed even though he genuinely had no idea what she was talking about. He thought briefly and concluded that what was missing at this moment was the use of common sense and creativity. It was apparent that this officer took her job very seriously and was doing the best she could in the fog of war. He needed only to give her some critical new information, and she would do her part, he thought.

"Officer, I have been instructed to tell you that this is not a terrorist attack. You have been an outstanding participant in today's activities which are a part of an exercise to test the town's defenses, and you have been brilliant. Let's all give the officer here a hand!" Homer turned toward the crowd behind him and held up his hand like a conductor. The crowd clapped and cheered.

"Frankly, Officer, I hope when you complete your service with the state that you would consider coming here to Grace and leading the premier criminal justice department in the area. So, thank you for your service, and let's end the exercise and reopen things. Good job!"

Homer proceeded to pull the baton out and open both of the doors. While the officer tried to understand what had just happened, Homer turned and addressed the growing crowd behind him.

"My fellow people of Grace. This morning Grace Comprehensive Hospital has successfully conducted a terrorist attack drill. It was so authentic that many people here in town thought that it was a real attack indeed. Please spread the word that we have scored in the

98th percentile for this event, but the exercise is now concluded. I want to again thank the officer beside me for her excellent supervision of the event. Thank you . . ." Homer struggled with the officer's name. "Officer, uh, Insky, I believe, for your excellent leadership this morning." The officer was still trying to process what had happened but graciously accepted the unexpected applause. But she was also increasingly distracted by a young man standing in front of her—the most handsome man she had ever seen. She felt compelled to move closer to him. Almost uncontrollably, the compulsion moved her ever so much closer to her tall, blond Viking warrior.

"Hello, I am Officer Brunhilde Dinsky."

"Hello, I am Mikhail Agapov." Their conversation ended at this point as the two introverted tall people looked longingly at each other but with absolutely no idea what to do next. The moment passed, and they both felt that they failed by not uttering a second sentence. But they were young, and there would be more chances down the road.

"Officer, is the sheriff okay?" asked Vladimir. He overlooked the apparent attraction between the officer and his oldest son.

"I do not know, sir. I haven't been back there to his room to check." She answered Vladimir without taking her eyes off of Mikhail. Mikhail, likewise, was locked onto Dinsky.

"Okay. Well, thank you. We will just have to wait here, I guess." Vladimir was a patient man. He stood in many bread lines in his youth in the Soviet Union. Homer was less patient.

"Well, let's go back and see." Homer pushed forward down the hall with Vladimir and Ludmilla in tow. Ludmilla was excited to be seeing her first Ebola case ever. The three walked toward the sheriff's

HOMER RESTORES ORDER—SORT OF

room but did not notice that Mikhail was not with them. Mikhail remained back at the double doors, about three feet from the officer. They were still staring at each other in silence. Homer pushed open the door to the sheriff's room and walked in. The other folks in the room stared at him with looks of puzzlement.

"Homer, why are you here?" Carl asked the familiar question, except on this occasion, it was in Sheriff Meeks' hospital room, not on Carl's front porch.

"I thought maybe I could be of some assistance," Homer offered.

"Well, Homer, it all started with your party yesterday," Sheriff Meeks said with a tinge of regret and more sobbing.

"Carl, explain to me what has transpired," Homer said.

"Well, it's a little tough to explain. You know about the llama and the pool and the sheriff's trip to the hospital, I guess. I had some business to discuss with the sheriff this morning. On the way, I was pulled over for speeding. The officer who pulled me over was from the State Bureau, and she is the one standing out in the hallway right now. Anyway, we got here, and I discussed some personal business with the sheriff. Unfortunately, he suffered a little problem that got blown way out of proportion—lots of excitement, people running around, and bells going off. So, someone misinterpreted all this as some sort of terrorist issue. Frankly, a series of unrelated things occurring in sequence led to the mistaken situation we find ourselves in."

Homer pondered the little story that Carl told while leaning on his walking stick. He thought through the various options then spoke with authority.

"Okay, well, we need to let folks know that there is no terrorist attack.

How best can we accomplish that?" Just as Homer finished his assessment of what should happen next, the door opened, and Betty stepped in. She looked at the men around the room and provided a rapid-fire evaluation.

"Boys, what kind of mess have you created this morning? I already sent the folks in the lobby home and just finished on the second floor. So, what's left to do?" Betty stood in the middle of the room, hands-on-hips, speaking with authority and firmness.

Carl, Sheriff Meeks, the nurses, and Homer looked at Betty but did not speak.

"Leave it to a woman to fix the mess you boys created!" Connie Marlboro, the fibrillating nurse, said without any particular insight into her role in the event. "You are right, Ms. Betty. A while ago, the two doctors came in, Dr. Hippo and Dr. Youseff, and said there was no Ebola! And no fibrillation, either!" Connie frowned at her last point, now realizing that maybe her original diagnosis was a little off. "But, you know, I think there was some of that. Maybe a little bit." Everyone looked at Connie, puzzled.

"Yep, they sure did! But I agree with my girl here," Meeks said while reaching up to a smiling Connie and patting her on the arm. "She saved my life, and I owe her dinner some time!" Connie blushed but was proud she could be of service. She wasn't sure if Meeks just asked her on a date or not.

Betty, Carl, and Homer looked at each other speechless and unable to fathom how this absurd situation evolved.

"Well, Ms. Betty, I think that my position here is no longer needed. I am going to head back to the estate. It was a shame you couldn't

HOMER RESTORES ORDER—SORT OF

make it to the celebration on Friday," Homer said.

"Homer, congratulations on your honor and your service to the town." Betty relaxed and put on her best and most gracious Southern charm. "Did you have a nice party?"

"Ms. Betty, it was delightful. Even with all the excitement!" Everyone looked at Sheriff Meeks, but he was still staring at Connie.

"Homer, I saw the video. When did you put those pink azaleas in by the pool?" Betty asked, having turned her attention to horticulture.

"Betty, you know, we did that just a few weeks ago. I was watching the Masters golf tournament on TV, and they just looked so nice that I went out and got a whole bunch."

"Well, Homer, they just look real fine, I tell you. Real fine." Betty answered, smiling. An absurd, disruptive morning at the hospital was ending as a pleasant discussion on the merits of southern azaleas.

"Ms. Betty, as always, it was delightful to see you, and please don't be a stranger," Homer said with a little peck on her outstretched hand as he exited.

And with that, the first terrorist attack in Grace was over. Sheriff Meeks agreed to the two-week notice, continued benefits for 12 months, and a plaque for more than twenty-five years of service. He also got Connie's cell number. Carl worked out the speeding violation with Officer Dinsky by inviting her to meet with him on Thursday to discuss the opening for the Sheriff's job. Homer exited the hospital to cheers from the remaining onlookers for saving Grace and ending the terrorist attack. He gave all the credit to Nursing Director Betty, who just shook her head and went to her office to do some paperwork. Ludmilla enjoyed the experience but realized that she would need to continue to learn about infectious diseases in nature. Having experienced a possible Ebola case for the first time, Ludmilla retired her mask, air pipe, bleach spray, and Halloween hazmat suit for now. She boxed her tools up and labeled the box "Grace Bioterror Attack— Maybe Ebola but Probably Not." The hazmat truck showed up from Atlanta, and at least as consolation, they gave Ludmilla a tour, a ride on the truck, and let her run some chemical tests. It reinforced her thoughts about the future and was pretty fun. She even quizzed the hazmat guys on their knowledge of Ebola, anthrax, and plague.

Major Lowman made it to the forest beside the hospital. He crouched under a clump of azaleas and did a ground-level visual assessment for terrorists, insurgents, and other revolutionaries. Then he waited to see if there was some action on the blockade he suggested. Deputy Jessup finally showed up at the hospital with no reinforcements and went inside for about five minutes. But then he came back out and drove away. No roadblocks or barricades, or perimeter fencing. Instead, Lowman saw Homer Pitts' limo pull up with a bunch of people piled in tight. Homer and his entourage entered the hospital, then came out about twenty minutes later, filed back into the limo, and drove away. Lowman could hear folks in the lobby clapping and cheering for Homer. So, while Lowman wasn't quite sure what was happening, he figured the event was probably just a false alarm.

But Major Lowman was curious and even suspicious about the role Homer played. Homer was neither an elected official nor a law enforcement officer, yet he seemed to have some authority in the event based on the crowd reaction. Lowman used his best deductive reasoning and concluded that Homer must be an essential part of

HOMER RESTORES ORDER—SORT OF

this, either as a domestic terrorism leader or a foreign spy probing the town's defenses. The whole thing may even have started at Homer's party when the sheriff was incapacitated. Well, Lowman figured he would need to conduct covert surveillance on Homer and his band of Russians. Try to find out if Homer was up to anything.

And on a romantic note, Dinsky and Mikhail connected. The connection was immediate and profound. They found a way to run into each other or drive by and wave each day. They were still trying to figure out how to take the next step in their budding romance. The next step was to have an actual conversation.

CHAPTER 6

SUPER ATHLETE AND INTREPID BUSINESSMAN, ALVIN TEABODY

"Alvin?" Homer's voice came over Alvin Teabody's cell phone.

"Homer," Alvin responded. Alvin was driving but had the phone on the car's sound system, so he didn't have to push any buttons.

"Dear sir, I have an idea," Homer said.

"Okay, Homer, I'm listening," Alvin answered.

"Tennis. Do you teach tennis?" Homer inquired.

"Of course. Why?" said Alvin.

"Can you come over to the house today, say, around 2 pm?" Homer asked.

"Okay," Alvin responded.

"Perfect. It will be worth your while," said Homer.

"Till then." Alvin hung up.

Alvin Teabody rolled back into his mansion in Grace in his silver 1989 Mercedes 560L. The car still ran like a charm. Even after a week sitting in the parking garage at Hartsfield-Jackson International Airport in Atlanta, the car started right up. It was a gift Alvin gave himself, bought during his last contract in professional football, before he went to Europe to play soccer—and way before he qualified for the senior professional golf tour or his summer in Bucharest learning tennis from some of the best. And before he won the Cincinnati Bowler's tournament on the way to six consecutive 300 games in Midwest tournaments. Alvin was fifty-eight years old now, and the days of his athletic exploits were behind him. His current income stream came from motivational seminars, books, and private coaching. He could coach or teach most sports through a combination of personal experiences, education, and training. These days, the foundation of his business empire was motivational talks he gave across the country. He gave the same inspirational ninety-minute guide to excellence two hundred times a year for a speaking fee plus expenses plus a royalty from ticket receipts. And parents ate it up. And then there was the Teabody Assessment for Sports Fit, which he and his wife, Contessa, created as his trademarked system for assessing which sport your child would excel in and what level they might achieve. Of course, he gave substantial discounts to poor but promising athletes and their families. And signed an agreement to receive a royalty payment if they made it to the big leagues.

Teabody owned a building in downtown Grace. Three stories, refurbished, and beautiful. Twelve staff. A separate gym and athletic field out back. Teabody's home was a few blocks away. A white Colonial-style, columned mansion with five bedrooms, 14-foot-tall ceilings, gorgeous hardwood floors, fireplaces, and a state-of-the-art renovated kitchen. Teabody had lived in some of the best places in the world but returned home to build his empire. He and Homer had that in common.

Alvin and Homer did well for two boys who nobody wanted back in 1972—ten-year-old friends, short, and not particularly good

SUPER ATHLETE AND INTREPID BUSINESSMAN, ALVIN TEABODY

at anything. There were thirteen boys in their class that first year of integrated schools. But only ten could play basketball at lunch. At ten, both Alvin and Homer were frail and unathletic. So, while the other boys played basketball, the two misfits would sit on a nearby bench for twenty minutes and talk, along with the third misfit, Gabriel Montcliff. Gabriel was the youngest member of the wealthiest family in town. He was the runt. Not particularly good at anything except empathy. He was a sweet boy who saw the best in people and suffered with them—a guppy to the sharks at home, living in the mansion that Homer would buy years later. Gabriel liked Homer and Alvin, and they liked him.

The three boys would talk about their families, the school, what they liked, and what they didn't. And what they wanted to be when they grew up. That twenty minutes together each day built their friendship. Not their families who lived on different sides of the railroad tracks. Just that twenty minutes a day of conversation. In later years, when Homer arrived in New York City, he would see Alvin play football. And when Homer had his first fashion show, Alvin was right there on the front row to see Homer's creations, seated between a leggy model and a sunglassed designer. And they both ended up back in Grace, with the two most prominent houses in town. Gabriel never made it out of Grace. He disappeared at age twelve and was never heard from again. Homer and Alvin had a suspicion of where he went, but no one would ever believe them.

Later that day.

"Mr. Teabody. Would you like sugar, lemon, or milk with your tea?" Mikhail asked, practicing for his coming days as a butler. He placed the Lenox china teacup and saucer on the glass table by the pool as Teabody sat down.

"A little lemon and one teaspoon of sugar. Thank you," Alvin responded politely.

"And I will bring you the Key lime pie in just a moment." After adding lemon and sugar to the tea, Mikhail placed the porcelain sugar bowl and silver spoon on the table next to the teacup. He disappeared back into the house and returned with a large slice of homemade pie. Homer arrived at the table and warmly embraced Alvin. Mikhail filled Homer's cup with freshly brewed Earl Grey along with a slice of lemon and two spoons of sugar. The air was warm and a little humid on the expansive, columned porch overlooking the Olympic pool as Homer and Alvin settled down to catch up, eat pie and do some business.

"Homer, sorry I missed your party yesterday, but I was finishing my tour in Los Angeles. Twenty cities, forty events, and 11,000 attendees. And I am just back this morning on the red-eye."

"Alvin, you should have told me this morning! We could have waited till tomorrow."

"No way. You're both a long-standing friend and a great customer, so you get the special treatment." Alvin raised his tea to Homer, accompanied by his effervescent trademark smile.

"How is the pie?" Homer asked. Valentina looked at several recipe books and online to find the perfect recipe, and then she made ten pies before she felt she had it just right. She added a few unique but secret ingredients to give it a special kick. Homer and Vladimir, and the rest of the family, were a little used to her special Key lime pie, but all agreed that she had mastered the pie, and it was the best they had ever tasted. Homer thought about commercializing her creation, but Valentina didn't want to share her ingredients. Homer engaged Alvin for another of his unique project ideas, and he wanted the Key lime to be fresh and the best Alvin ever tasted.

"Best I ever tasted. Where, oh where, did you get this?"

"It's from the loving hands of Valentina right here in our kitchen!"

"How about a second piece? About half that size." Alvin was a picky eater. He had to be. At 58, he didn't need any extra pounds hanging around. It would hurt his image as a fitness and sports consultant and trainer. His asking for a second piece, well, that just put a shine on the whole pie-making journey for Valentina.

"Wow, of course," Homer answered, and he summoned Valentina to bring a second piece and receive praise from Alvin directly. She took a bow and smiled effusively. Then it was down to business.

"Alvin, I have a proposition and a question. First, the proposition. I want you to consider training a group of young women to be world-class championship tennis players. They will be beginners, but my instincts tell me that they will learn fast."

"Okay. And the question?" Alvin answered.

"How long would it take?" Homer asked.

"Do the girls have any experience with tennis at all?" Alvin asked.

"No," Homer responded.

"Athletically inclined?" Alvin asked.

"Yes," Homer responded briskly.

"And where are they located?"

"Here. It's the Agapov girls. They have Russian blood and long, strong legs. I believe they will be world-class tennis players."

"Well, I will see. I need to do some testing first, then some physical training before getting the girls on the courts. By the way, are we going to do this out here or over at the YMCA courts?"

"Here. I will have Mr. Agapov build a court."

"Courts. How many girls?"

"Six."

"Build three courts then. They will learn first by playing with each other and with me. We will also need floodlights for nighttime practice, especially on hot, humid summer days. Six lights. One each on the corners and two in the middle. On poles up about twenty feet. How long do you think it will take to do that?"

"Maybe a week? I will have Vladimir start the work today."

"Okay. Let's plan to start the lessons in two weeks, so have the courts ready by then. Next week, I will come out and do athletic testing and start the physical training. All in all, I think six months of my training should be able to tell us if they are champions or not. Now, let's talk about what happened yesterday. I heard all the way out in California about a terrorist attack."

"Alvin, it was a comedy of errors. The mayor, sheriff, an out-of-town state bureau agent, and a variety of bit players. But, exciting, I guess. All started with the video."

"Yeah, I saw that at the airport waiting on my flight. Wacky! Was that Meeks on the llama?

"In all his glory! Yesterday, everything got wacky and mangled at the hospital, triggering the insane thought that a terrorist attack was underway. And it took the good sense of Betty Gilroy to ask a few sensible questions and get things settled down. I arrived at the event late but tried to help Betty assuage fears and trepidation amongst our good townsfolk."

"So, I heard that the sheriff is going to retire?"

"Yep, and I think Deputy Jessup will take over temporarily."

"Hmm. Interesting," Alvin said. A new sheriff might offer an opportunity for some new business with the town, Alvin calculated. But Jessup was a lackluster candidate, he thought. "Any other news, Homer?"

"Not really. I think we are all a little taxed out from yesterday's drama."

"You didn't even ask how much the training of tennis champions would cost?" Alvin questioned.

"Well, I figure if you have to ask, you can't afford it. Anyway, I know that you will give me a 30% discount as a friend."

"Of course, and if you ask for a price now, then you will know if you get the discount at checkout or not, right?"

"Bingo. I would just rather believe in the discount and pay whatever you bill me. It's called trust."

"To friendship and trust!" Alvin raised his teacup and clinked it with Homer's. This was how their relationship had been over the last 40-plus years.

CHAPTER 7

A BACKGROUND INVESTIGATION BEGINS

Captain Monroe Elliott sat in a leather seat in the Delta Sky Lounge at Newark International Airport, waiting for the noon flight to Atlanta. He sipped his second orange juice as he waited and flipped through his texts and emails. Grace, Georgia was a bit over an hour north of the Atlanta airport. He reserved a rental car for when he arrived, an Audi Q3. In the sight of the mountains but still primarily flat farmland and some rolling hills, a river ran through the town of Grace. He would take the I-285 ring road around Atlanta then up I-75 north toward Chattanooga. The Captain had previously lived in Atlanta for eighteen months about fifteen years earlier. But he hadn't been back in a long time, and the city had grown impressively. Like a growing blob absorbing farmland and woods, ranch houses that weren't in fashion anymore, and old shopping centers replacing all that with gleaming new towers, colossal distribution centers, and neighborhoods with rows of mini-mansions on postage-stamp-sized lots.

"Good afternoon. May I have your attention, please? Flight 2025 to Atlanta is now boarding. Would the first class passengers please approach the boarding gate." The Captain pulled out his iPhone and brought up his e-ticket. Once he scanned through at the gate, he headed to seat 2A. He secured his carry-on and handed his jacket to the attendant and ordered for a gin and tonic. He would arrive in Atlanta midafternoon, and by the time he headed up I-75, he would have lost any of the effects of the gin. So one drink would just let him catch up on some shut-eye on the flight down. The seat next to him was empty, the flight was only half full. The Captain hoped it would be a quiet flight as he leaned back right after takeoff and closed his eyes. He slept soundly for the next two hours. The attendant saw that the Captain was sleeping soundly and gave the gin and tonic to another passenger.

The landing was smooth. Captain Elliott only woke up when the attendant gently pressed his shoulder after landing, and the other passengers had disembarked. He was the last one on the plane. The Captain thanked the attendants and pilots, grabbed his carry-on, and hurried off the plane. Once inside Terminal B, he headed down the escalator to the tram and rode it to the main terminal, where he quickly found the rental car kiosk and he was off. The interstate was pretty open, so he made a good time around Atlanta and up toward Chattanooga. He passed several exits and finally turned off toward Grace. Ten miles off the interstate to get to the town limits and the only hotel in town, The Grace Inn. Forty rooms and breakfast in the morning. It wasn't part of a chain but instead was locally owned and run. It appeared to be about half full judging from the parking lot, which positively surprised the Captain. Small town, mid-week with nothing special going on, and still pretty full. He strode up to the Counter to check-in.

"Welcome to the Grace Inn, the only hotel in Grace," the short, plump, middle-aged lady behind the counter said while smiling sweetly. "How can I help you?" She now had the computer screen pulled up for check-in.

A BACKGROUND INVESTIGATION BEGINS

"Good afternoon. I am Captain Monroe Elliot, and I reserved a room for the next two nights in your fine establishment."

"Oooh, honey, I like the way you talk. Smooth." She punched a few keys and pulled up the reservation. "We have you in the Presidential Suite. There is one king bed in the bedroom and a living room with a 60-inch TV, sofa, easy chair, microwave, and mini-bar. We have a hot breakfast bar from 6 a.m. to 10 a.m. And the English tea hour is from 4 to 6. It's two hours," she said, giggling at her little joke.

"Well, thank you, my dear. Sounds delightful."

"Oooh. I like the way that sounds." Her smile was from ear to ear now.

Captain Elliot signed the voucher for the two nights and gave the lady at the counter a wink as he walked away. A quick ride up the elevator and ten steps to his room. He went in and flipped the lights on. The room was as advertised and better than he expected. He took a quick shower, dressed in some casual clothes, and went back downstairs. He had a couple of meetings set up before dinner, so he went quickly to his car. But not before a shout-out from the desk clerk. "Have a good time, sugar!"

"Major Lowman, it's good to see you again after all these years."

"You too, Captain Elliot. How can I help you?"

"I am here to conduct a very discreet and sensitive investigation. I work for a London firm that may want to do some business with Mr. Homer Pitts, but we need to know a little more about him." Elliot was upfront and very professional. He had the Major sign a very lengthy non-disclosure agreement, and he gave the major a fee schedule depending on the amount of helpful information provided and the time spent. The major was suspicious from the start. This seemed to him to be like a National Security investigation, and he figured that the US government might be on Homer's trail. So, the major felt compelled to share everything as he saw it.

"Well, it's my professional opinion as a former military man that Mr. Homer Pitts is probably a foreign operative. He has a house full of Russians, and just yesterday, he had a very central role in our town's first terrorist attack, out at the hospital."

"Terrorist attack? I didn't see anything in the national press about that."

"Yes, it's the power of Homer Pitts that he can suppress such an important story."

"I see. How long have you known Homer?"

"Since last fall. I have interacted with him a little bit, but nothing major."

"Is he involved in any types of shady business or criminal activity?"

"No, I don't think so."

The interview went on for about thirty minutes. Nothing of substance emerged other than Major Lowman's strong opinions, right or wrong. The skilled investigator learned that Homer, for all his quirks, was a decent fellow who energetically pursued life and that the people around him, including the Russians, were also pretty decent folks. The Captain thanked the major and excused himself.

Captain Elliot next drove to City Hall for a pre-arranged appointment with the mayor. Carl was waiting in his comfortable office in the southwest corner of the second floor of the building. The office was known to have a nice view of the sunset with no obstruction. Carl never worked late enough to see a sunset, even in the winter. When Elliot arrived, Carl's secretary led the Captain in and sat him down in the wing chair across from Carl.

A BACKGROUND INVESTIGATION BEGINS

"Good afternoon, Captain. How can I help you?"

"Well, hello Mayor, and thank you again. I know I was terse over the phone, but in short, a London firm has engaged me to conduct a background investigation on a Mr. Homer Pitts. I have exhausted all research available on the internet, so now I am conducting interviews. I spoke with Major Lowman, the town historian, and now I'd like to talk with you.

"Why?"

"The firm may want to do some business with Mr. Pitts, but they need to do due diligence to move forward."

"I see. Well, have you talked to Mr. Pitts?"

"In short, yes. Our staff contacted him last evening. He signed this release to talk candidly with you, and I am scheduled to meet with him tomorrow over dinner at his home." The Captain slid the authorization form across the table for the mayor to inspect. Carl glanced at the paper, then turned his attention to the Captain.

"Well, what would you like to know?"

"How long have you known Mr. Pitts?"

Carl was a year ahead of Homer and Lula Bell, who were in the third grade. Carl noticed Homer, a small, quiet kid, but Carl didn't think much of him until Homer ran for class president against Carl in the twelfth grade. Homer was intelligent, and he skipped the 9th grade. Homer read in a book that the 9th grade was the most challenging grade of all. Big adjustment for kids coming from middle school. Hormones, dealing with the 12th graders, career or college expectations, and a state requirement to earn enough credits to graduate. Homer made his mind up in the 5th grade that the 9th grade was the one to skip, and he planned accordingly. He opted out of PE so he could take an extra math class. Homer told the principal that he had palpitations every time he exercised, and his doctor could not refute it. So, the principal decided to let Homer take more math and skip exercise. And then there was 9th grade English. He tested out of 8th grade English and got to join the 9th-grade class a year early. And in those days, there was still only one school in Grace, so it wasn't too hard to walk across the hall and be a 9th grader for one period. It all added up, and pretty soon, he had enough high school credits while still in middle school to skip the 9th grade, which meant that Homer and Carl faced off for the presidency a couple of years later.

Homer didn't stand a chance. The foundation of Homer's platform was that he was more intelligent than Carl, as evidenced by his accelerated educational course. But Carl was taller, more athletic, and more handsome. He possessed a better, deeper voice, was the Captain of the State Championship football team and was dating a beauty queen, Miss Lula Bell. But Homer had a secret weapon. Challenges. He had read a book about challenges to voting and how to overturn an election. He also read about negotiating tactics.

"I have known of Mr. Pitts since he was in the third grade, but I really got to know him as a senior in high school. So, about forty years." Carl figured that the investigator only needed to know how long and not the nature of the relationship. He was wrong.

"And what was the nature of your relationship in high school, Mr. Longfellow."

"Well, we both ran for class president. I won." Carl proudly recounted.

"My understanding is that Mr. Pitts contested the election. Is that right?"

Carl was dumbfounded. How did the investigator find that out?

A BACKGROUND INVESTIGATION BEGINS

"Well, contested is a mighty strong word. It was more like he wanted to know the vote total."

"Do you remember the vote total?"

"I believe it was 19-1, for me."

"And what was the basis of Mr. Pitts's complaint?"

"He said that the ballots were confusing and that the 19 votes were meant for him."

"Was that true?" Elliott asked.

"No, and on the second ballot, redone to ensure that it was clear, the total was 19-1 for me, again."

"And the third ballot? What was the basis for that?" the Captain asked.

The Captain had done his homework. Carl was impressed.

"When the second ballot was cast, the fire alarm went off. It happened to be when Homer stepped out to use the restroom. We never knew who pulled the fire alarm. I had a suspicion. So he challenged the ballot based on the interruption. Homer's ballot was the only ballot missing before the alarm went off."

"And did you win on the third ballot?"

"Yes. But Homer didn't challenge that one because we came to an accommodation."

"Which was?"

"We allowed Homer to serve as the 2nd President. He wanted Co-President. I said Vice President. But, finally, we settled on the 2nd President. It left things a little open to interpretation, which Homer liked. It could mean a lot of things. If he put "class president" on his resume, it was technically true. Homer had studied negotiation at night and listened to this expert on AM radio every day, so I knew he might keep this going and use up our only senior year without a resolution. I figured I needed to get this settled somehow. I was the politician, you see. He was an activist. But we were fairly good at getting to a compromise in those days."

"Mayor, would you say that Mr. Pitts is energetic, industrious, and a go-getter?"

"Definitely. When Homer wants something, he goes after it." Carl said. He didn't know where this was going, and he was still friends with Homer, so he wanted to try to be helpful where he could.

The Captain went through most of the significant events in Homer's life, and the Mayor shared what he knew, good and bad. It took about an hour. Then the last question caught the Mayor by surprise.

"Mayor, do you know if Mr. Pitts has ever been to Switzerland?" Elliot asked.

"No, I don't know for sure, but I don't think he has. At least, he has never told me he has."

"Thank you, Mr. Mayor. You have been quite helpful." Elliot replied. He left and had an early dinner at the hotel, then turned in to catch up on his sleep. The following day Captain Elliott snooped around town most of the day, picking up little details here and there on Homer. Before leaving on a late evening flight, he planned to have an early dinner with Homer at his estate to finish up his assessment.

CHAPTER 8

THE SUMMER OF 1963

"Her eyes sparkled blue like gorgeous sapphires," Count Armand St. Clare said to his young assistant. "I was a young account executive when I noticed her, first on the subway, then at the Gemstone Diner in downtown Manhattan. Two blocks over from my office and on the way from my usual subway stop. The first time she served me at the diner, I sat in the back booth looking out over the street. I had a copy of the Wall Street Journal and was on page 18 reading a story about an Italian company selling out to a French conglomerate when she came over. I remember it like it was yesterday, and it was nearly sixty years ago." The nostalgic Count paused for a few moments to compose himself. He decided to keep the rest of the story in his heart without sharing it with the assistant. But he remembered.

"Good morning. Will you be having coffee today?" the young waitress had asked him that fateful morning, with a charming Southern accent.

He had looked up from his paper. Usually, he just barked out his order to a waitress. But for some reason, he looked up at this one. Her eyes he'd noticed first—Blue, like the waters of the Cote d'Azur. Then the natural, golden-blond hair fell down both sides of her tender, tanned face. Her smile—bright and toothy. Two dimples like exclamations, framing her happy smile. She had a long slender neck, a curvy body, and two long, shapely legs peeking out from her short waitress skirt. And her lean arms and hands. He couldn't speak, which was unusual for a sophisticated European and recent Harvard graduate who relocated to his family's firm in Manhattan. She smiled and finally said to him, "What's the matter, honey? Cat got your tongue?"

Her accent entranced him. Everything about her bewitched him. He finally spoke, slowly.

"Two boiled eggs, toast with butter and orange marmalade, and one link of pork sausage."

"Okay, that's better. Coming right up. Coffee too?"

"Yes. And orange juice."

"Fresh squeezed?"

For a brief moment, he imagined squeezing her. His vivid imagination was working overtime, and it was 7:30 in the morning, before work. When he didn't answer, she answered for him.

"Yes, freshly squeezed for you!" she said with a wink. "By the way, my name is Angelina. What's yours?"

"Armand."

"That's a nice name, and both of our names start with an "A." Isn't that sweet!"

Their first date was a week later. They went to an Italian restaurant, shared pizza, and drank a bottle of chianti. He walked her back to the apartment she was renting with two other girls. Polite, friendly, a little peck on the cheek. A colleague of Armand's, Gustavo Faubert, asked Angelina out as well. But, Angelina turned Gustavo down. She

THE SUMMER OF 1963

liked Armand much better. Gustavo was incensed.

Angelina and Armand saw each other again the next night. And again. It was 1963; the ban on *Lady Chatterley's Lover* was lifted, the pill was on the way, and the Beatles were getting hot. For the next month, Angelina and Armand spent evenings and weekends together and achieved a level of intimacy that would usually require marriage in earlier days. For most people—but not Angelina. She had already been married. When the Count bought her that beautiful black dress and they went to the party at the private club atop a Manhattan skyscraper, she knew she was falling in love. They spent the night together at the Waldorf. She felt like heaven. And they were intimate. Physically, yes, but also emotionally at a level she didn't know was possible. She knew then how love could feel. The past months had been the best in her short life.

But they were from different worlds. Angelina knew inside that she couldn't fit into Armand's world, that it would be heartache for them both. Not right away, but someday. And the breakup later would be more challenging, uglier. She made up her mind to be thankful for a few months of joy in life, a joy that would never be forgotten nor taken away.

The following day, she eased quietly out of bed and the hotel room and out of Armand's life. The note only said that she would always love him and not to look for her. To say that the Count was heartbroken would be to minimize the pain he felt. He would look for her for the decades to come but would never find her. Only a few letters would continue to connect them—all with no return address postmarked from Atlanta. Angelina told him that she was from Atlanta, but after years of searching, he never found her.

CHAPTER 9

DECISIONS AND DINNER

The following day Homer decided to have a heart-to-heart with the Agapov parents and instruct them on the planned evening and dinner guest.

"Vladimir and Valentina, it's time for us to think about the future of your children. Now let's start with Mikhail. What do you think about butler's school?" Homer asked as the three took a mid-morning coffee break together.

"I want him to do what he wants to do, to be a man, and to have a family," declared Vladimir. "He is a good boy, smart, and if being a manservant is what he wants, then okay."

"Vladimir, a butler is more than a manservant. Yes, you serve, but at the level that Mikhail is capable of, it is quite a job and pays well. What about you, Valentina?"

Valentina was sentimental and had a big heart. Her eyes welled up with tears.

"Babushka. I want to be a babushka. Mikhail is at home here with little children and a wife. Yes, that sounds okay to me." Valentina pulled out a wadded-up handkerchief to wipe her eyes, now filled with abundant tears.

Homer was struck by how Vladimir and Valentina gave up their careers and the land of their birth to give their children an opportunity at something better. Yet, they put no pressure on their children to be doctors, lawyers, scientists, or entrepreneurs. Just be happy. Homer was even more committed to helping them achieve what they wanted.

"Okay. I checked into the school Mikhail mentioned. I called a few friends in Europe. It checks out, and it is the best in the world. He seems to have done his homework. He will have to go for at least a month, but a friend in London suggested that he take a six-month internship at a European estate and finish the ten-day course in St. Petersburg. Then he should be ready to handle whatever is required to get his Queen's certificate. I will pay the expenses for it all. I, too, just want him to be happy. We need to work with him on the application, but the course will start in June if all goes well."

Vladimir and Valentina exploded out of their chairs with hugs around Mr. Homer's neck, and, of course, Valentina shed even more tears of happiness. The following conversation would be a little more complicated.

"Okay, so we have a plan for Mikhail. So next, what about the girls. Have you thought about a plan for them?"

"Grandchildren?" Valentina asked tentatively.

"Okay, but they need a husband for that. Do you want them to do anything else?"

"They are good workers. I think they can work at the antique mall." Vladimir was a little constrained in his aspirations for them.

"Okay. Well, I have been giving it some thought. I noticed at the

DECISIONS AND DINNER

▲

party when they were running around in their bathing suits that your girls are quite athletic, speedy, and strong. And then Sunday night, I saw an advertisement for the Wimbledon tennis tournament in June. And I thought, Russian girls and tennis. Maybe they should try tennis? What do you think?"

Vladimir and Valentina looked at each other then back at Homer.

"Tennis? How?" Vladimir spoke for them both.

"I have a friend, Alvin Teabody, who is a trainer of sports champions. He has agreed to train them."

"Yes, Mr. Teabody is quite famous and a master of many sports. He drives the Mercedes and has a beautiful home in town," Vladimir acknowledged.

"Well, he will assess their talent and potential, then if any of the girls seem to be good candidates for tennis, he can coach them. Or find someone to coach them who is at the top of the game."

"Tennis stars?" Valentina murmured. The idea was beginning to register, and she was warming to its potential. But Valentina was also concerned about the possibility of grandchildren. She kept the thoughts about grandchildren to herself, at least for now.

"Mister Homer. What about when our Mikhail comes back from his training? Will he be able to have a little home for his own?" Valentina blurted out.

"Valentina, you are wise to consider this. So that leads me to the last thing to discuss. We need to build a house for Mikhail and tennis courts for the girls. Vladimir, are you up to this challenge?"

Vladimir thought for a moment. He would have Mikhail a little bit longer to help with the courts before leaving for school. And it was time for Boris to learn some home-building skills when Mikhail left. Vladimir didn't know how to build a tennis court, but he could consult YouTube, he thought. And Mr. Homer would pay for all the materials.

"Yes, Mr. Homer. I can do it all."

"Okay, then. We have a deal." Everyone was happy, for now. But construction projects always had a way of uncovering the unexpected.

Later, Homer gave instructions to the Agapovs in preparation for Captain Elliot's arrival.

"The Captain will be here at 7 p.m., so let's plan to have drinks, appetizers, the first course, clear the table, and let him and I talk a bit, then the second course followed by dessert and coffee on the patio."

"Yes, Mr. Homer. We will be ready," Valentina and Mikhail replied.

Homer received reports from each of the people with whom the Captain spoke. The questions were general and aimed at whether Homer was good, honest, and trustworthy—any skeletons in his closet? But nothing as to what the whole thing was about.

By midafternoon, Homer placed some calls.

"Lucius, I would like for you to come by this evening around 7 p.m., for dinner. I have a guest coming, and I may need your expertise."

"Sure, Homer. I will be there." Lucious Marlowe responded with a slow Southern drawl that obscured his Ivy League credentials. He was the best lawyer around, whatever the issue was. Lucious could handle pretty much any kind of case or conversation, and he knew the best technical talent to pull in when he needed help. Based in the North Atlanta suburbs, he enjoyed the drive up to Grace. He was a country boy at heart.

"What do you think he is interested in?" Lucious asked.

DECISIONS AND DINNER

"I don't rightly know, Lucious," Homer responded. "He seems to be asking many questions about my morals mostly, but no one knows why. But if it's important enough for him to fly down from New York for a couple of days, I want to be prepared."

"Okay. How are your finances?" Lucious inquired, gently.

"I think they're fine, but I haven't talked to Sam in a while."

"Talk to him before dinner. Make sure you know where you stand."

"Okay," Homer said.

"Later." Lucious hung up.

Homer looked through his contacts to find his financial manager's number. Homer hadn't spoken to Sam in quite a while, although Sam had left several voicemails and sent emails imploring Homer to get in touch.

"Sam Klein speaking."

"Sam, this is Homer. How are you?"

"Fine. You?" Sam answered cautiously.

"Fine. I have an out-of-town guest coming for dinner tonight. It's business, and I need to be prepared to state my financial position. So, I am calling to find out how it is?"

"Glad you finally called, Homer, because I needed to talk to you anyway," an exasperated Sam barked out at Homer. "I have been telling you for some time now to slow down your spending. Your fortune is almost gone. Your mutual fund returns are mostly down. Your rental properties have more vacancies than usual, so rental income is down too. And your royalty income is down. Well, nonexistent. You haven't published anything in over three years, ever since you came back to Grace. So your net worth is still not bad on paper because of your land holdings, but you are going to need to cultivate some new revenue sources, or you are going to need to sell all your real estate."

"Okay. I like it straight up, and that's pretty straight. Should I be worried?"

"Homer, you don't hear me, do you. I think that's the problem. You have selective hearing. Homer, I know it's just you now. Your mother is gone. You don't have a spouse or children to consider, so you might think you are okay. But, frankly, you should have been worried a year ago. Now, you should panic."

"Thanks for the thought, Sam. I will keep it in mind." Homer responded, apparently oblivious to Sam's concern.

"Okay, what time do you want me there?" Sam asked. Homer hadn't invited Sam for dinner, but as he thought about it, Homer realized that if a question did come up about finances, it might be better to have Sam answer than to put himself on the spot.

"Seven. Come around seven," Homer responded.

"See you then," Sam said as he hung up.

Homer needed to hear what Sam said even though he didn't want it to be true. There was one thing Sam got wrong, though. For Homer, it wasn't just him. It was the Agapovs, the ladies reading club, the antique mall. It was everyone in Grace for whom he felt a responsibility. He would have to figure it out. But that was for another day. Today, he needed to concentrate on the visit.

Homer called the Captain.

"Captain, I am looking forward to meeting you at the house around 7 p.m. I want to include a couple of other folks at dinner—my lawyer and my finance manager. Will that be okay with you?"

DECISIONS AND DINNER

"Sure. The more, the merrier. See you then."

Homer got up from his chair in the study and walked into the kitchen to tell Valentina.

"Let's add two more settings for dinner, Valentina."

"Yes, Mr. Homer."

At the hotel, the Captain laid back on the bed. He had the TV turned to one of the local channels watching the early news. School board meetings, a cow loose on the highway, a church scandal. He glanced at the news occasionally for some local flavor but mostly worked on his report. The Captain learned so far, in two days, that Homer was an unusual guy but decent. At Homer's dinner, he wanted to see if Homer fit the expected profile and also had to get a saliva sample. Homer's interest in spitting might come in handy for that. As the Captain was finishing the report, he drifted off to sleep.

"Wake-up call for Mr. Elliott."

"Okay, thanks very much." The Captain looked at the clock on the side table. After a quick shower, Captain Elliot put on a set of fresh clothes and headed out, dropping his key and some thanks at the front desk. He drove off toward Homer's estate, which was about six miles away. On the way, he noticed that the gas tank was near empty, so he stopped at a poorly-lit gas station. After filling up, he saw that the credit card reader wasn't working, so he went in to pay.

Inside the station, there was nobody at the cash register. He looked at his watch and saw that he had 15 minutes to get to Homer's. He waited for a few minutes, but no one came to the counter. Getting irritable, he plopped down a twenty-dollar bill to cover the $13.56 bill and walked back out to his car.

As the Captain walked toward his car, the door to the gas station behind him opened wildly, and a man ran out, headed toward a car on the opposite end of the parking lot. Dressed in blue jeans, cowboy boots and hat, and a blue sequin-studded shirt, he ran past the Captain, the parked car, and into the woods across the street. The Captain turned back toward the gas station door to see a sixtyish, gray-haired woman come running out with a sawed-off, side-by-side, double-barreled shotgun. She let both barrels fire toward the running man. He kept running, and she broke open the gun and reloaded. It was only then that she saw the Captain frozen in the middle of the parking lot. The Captain was a combat veteran, but this was something different. He looked at her with wide-open eyes but uttered no sounds. She looked at him and smiled. He could see that she had at least one gold tooth and very few of her natural teeth. She whipped around and headed back inside without saying a word.

The Captain wasn't quite sure what to do next. Should he go back in and let her know the twenty was his and that he, indeed, had paid for his gas? Or should he walk the fifty feet to his rental car and head out, hoping that no buckshot flew his way? He contemplated the two choices for what seemed like an eternity. He was already running late, but something pulled him back inside. Call it curiosity. So, he cautiously approached the door. As he put his hands on the door, he could see the lady behind the register and bulletproof glass. He headed in the door and looked at her.

"This your twenty, mister?" she asked.

"Yes."

"Want your change?" She looked at him with a stare that sent

DECISIONS AND DINNER

▲

a cold chill through him. She was menacing in her appearance. He didn't think delaying his exit was worth $6.44 in change.

"You keep it." He headed out the door and didn't look back. It would take him eighteen seconds to reach the car. He thought he heard the door open behind him again, so he took off running to close the distance. He didn't turn around or look back. He just kept going. He made it to the car and jumped in. Out he pulled, and down the road, he went. He never looked back at the gas station and put as much distance between him and the station as possible. He left so quickly that he lost his bearings and was soon out into an unfamiliar area. And he just kept driving until, at 7:15 pm, he realized that he was no longer in Grace, and in the fading sunlight, he was somewhere on the road driving through a forest. But he was a man, and stopping to get his bearings wasn't in the cards. He just kept driving and trusted his "sixth sense." Many men have this ability or believe they do. No maps, no GPS, no asking for directions. Just trust your directional sense. Around 7:30, he crossed over into Alabama, which he knew was not the right direction. He was lost and getting "loster" by the minute. He finally called Homer and pleaded guilty to getting lost. Homer listened intently to the description the Captain gave and responded expertly.

"Sir," Homer said, "at the next intersection, turn left. Go fourteen miles until you see the Crossroads Primitive Baptist Church on the right. It's wooden and painted white. There, you turn left again. You will head down a winding dirt road for 2 miles. At the secondary road, you come to turn left again. Follow that road 21 miles, and you will end up at my house on the left. I will have someone out there waiting for you. It should take you 45 minutes. See you then."

The Captain was a bit shell-shocked but somehow remembered the directions. As he approached the mansion, it finally dawned on him that he could have just used the map on his iPhone. But the unexpected terror at the gas station wiped his brain of any logical thoughts for a while, and GPS was a little spotty anyway. He slowed down as the grand front yard came into view. A tall young man waited at the driveway. The Captain slowed down and opened the window to talk to the young man.

"Hello sir, I am Mikhail. I will escort you to the parking area."

"Thank you. I will just follow you, right?"

"Yes, just follow me."

Wearing a tuxedo, Mikhail hopped into a golf cart and drove down the long driveway with the Captain behind him until they got to the parking area. Mikhail waited as the Captain got his briefcase out of the trunk then escorted him inside. The Captain was impressed with the young man's courtesy and grace. He spoke English with a Russian accent. Captain Elliot was intrigued as they walked through the walnut-paneled entry hall toward the living room, looking out over the back acreage. The living room was filled with what appeared to be heirloom antique furniture and dominated by a large marble fireplace. They headed through a pair of French doors onto the flagstone patio from the living room, where three well-dressed gentlemen sat laughing. A thick white tablecloth covered the wrought iron table where they sat. Three candles glowed in the middle of the table.

Drinks and a set of half-eaten appetizers were on the table. The men stood up as the Captain approached. The lawyer shook hands first, then the financial advisor and last was Homer, who stood across

DECISIONS AND DINNER

from the Captain. After introductions and pleasantries, Captain Elliot tried to explain what had happened. After a few minutes, laughter and knowing glances filled the table.

"That woman is my third cousin—one of the Pitts!" Homer said laughingly. "Aren't many of them left! A pretty violent crowd and mean to boot. You are lucky she didn't shoot you in the back just for fun." Captain Elliot smiled and acknowledged that the local color might be a helpful context in the report.

The mention of his third cousin brought a momentary flashback to Homer from childhood--of the screaming and beatings that he and his mama endured. Homer and Mama called her husband the Old Man. He was mean when he was sober and worse when he was drunk, which was his state a great deal of the time. His three sons from his previous marriage were chips off the old block. Mama finally had enough and divorced him for good when Homer left for New York City. She thought Homer would finally be safe from the Pitts in New York, and she moved out to live out her life in a small house in town. Happier, but still poor. And she never left Grace. At least as far as Homer knew.

The Captain felt at home with Homer, as if with old friends, although it was an environment new to him and with people until he had never met this night. By the end of the dinner two hours later, Homer had convinced the Captain to spend the night and arranged for his airline reservation to be moved to the following day. The Captain and Homer talked until midnight. And the next day, as he left, the customarily reserved Captain hugged his new friend, Homer. It was that kind of evening. They even talked about Homer's financial woes. Good cop, bad cop. Sam painted a picture of the disaster, and

Homer had a sparkling answer for every concern. Sam was skeptical, but the Captain could see Homer's unmistakable creativity and knew more about Homer's future than any of the other men at the table, including Homer. So the Captain was not as concerned as Sam.

On the flight back to New York, Captain Elliot finished writing his report on his laptop. He took a nap. Landing just before lunch, he headed straight over to his office to call Archie in London.

"Archie, sorry I am calling you late," the Captain said.

"Captain, how was your flight back?" Archie asked.

"Good. I intended to come late last night, but I spent a delightful evening at Homer's and ended up spending the night."

"Really. So objectively, what do you think?"

"Swell chap—Smart, broad-minded, cultured, funny. Impressed me," the Captain replied.

"Okay. Good to know. I assume you will write a full report?"

"Written and submitted already. I also have the specimen I took from Homer's wineglass and will take it over to the lab shortly."

"Do you think that Homer has the characteristics that we will be seeking?" Archie asked vaguely.

"Yes. Most definitely. Homer has creativity, panache, and a good heart," the Captain said, and he was pretty sure. "He could use some help with money management, but in this situation, I don't think that's an immediate concern."

Archie and the Captain talked a bit longer, and then Archie hung up. Archie looked online and skimmed through the report, jotting down a few critical comments or questions left to answer. Then he called Switzerland to talk to the Count.

DECISIONS AND DINNER

"The Captain is back in New York, and we just spoke. Mr. Pitts checks out. He seems like a very clever fellow, and he has strong traits that you will find familiar. We need to get the test results back, but that should take only a few days. I think we should move forward with an invitation and schedule the visit for a time in the next few weeks."

"A formal report is available, I assume?" the Count asked.

"Yes, everything is written up that is currently available. I just sent it by secure email to your account."

"Okay. I will have my staff here prepare for the visit. And you think he should come here, do you?" the Count asked.

"Yes. He should experience firsthand the gravity of this situation."

"Okay. Let's move forward, shall we?"

"Right-o."

The short conversation was to the point. The invitation to travel to Switzerland would be in two weeks. And the critical test would be available well before the trip. This would be Homer's first trip to Switzerland, and he would have much to digest and learn if this whole plan was to work. But it was imperative, from the good Count's perspective, for it to work.

CHAPTER 10

▲

A NEW VENTURE

Homer still didn't know why the Captain came to Grace. Something about a business opportunity that was potentially available but with no details and yet so important to warrant a trip from New York. It sounded like maybe it was a scam. But at least, it was a sophisticated one. And at least he had his financial and legal advisors involved from the beginning. He tried to put it out of his mind, which happened once his thoughts turned back to his personal financial affairs.

After talking more extensively with Sam, Homer finally accepted that the only profitable revenue streams were publication royalties, which were now practically nil. Sam and he discussed writing some articles and maybe even a book. Celebrity gossip and revealing secrets didn't appeal to Homer anymore, and, ethically, he was against it. Could he write a novel based loosely on his life? Maybe, but Sam thought the path to publication might be more tortuous now that Homer had been away from New York for a while. He could cut back on his donations to various town activities, but that would hurt some good people, and it wasn't where the bulk of his spending was going anyway. No, the excess expenditure mainly was the estate, including what he provided the Agapovs.

After Sam left and the Captain had retired to sleep, Homer walked out into the night air and, looking over his estate in the moonlight, and began to hatch a new idea. A working estate. A destination estate. With the Agapovs, he had a built-in workforce.

The following day, Homer got up early and rode out to visit with Mama. Her grave was out on the east side of town, in the rather extensive Grace Memorial Gardens. Well run, the Gardens were managed by the Bellamy brothers. They were very responsible businessmen who fully funded the trust that kept the cemetery in excellent shape. Mama had been quite clear that she didn't want to be buried underground. She didn't like the idea of worms eating her up. But at first, Mama wasn't warm to being put in a mausoleum at the Gardens. The Gardens occupied land that previously hosted a triple X-rated drive-in theatre showing nudie films after 10 p.m. Homer had several conversations with her invoking historical examples to convince her that a previous sin wouldn't permanently stain the land. She finally gave in and let Homer make her arrangements before she died. He built her a nice granite mausoleum with an artistic memorial plaque that included a porcelain picture of her. And beside her was a spot for him when that day came. The Rudyard Kipling poem "If" was etched into the wall facing her tomb, with the words altered to be appropriate for a woman and not a man. All fashioned by Homer and ready the week before she died. On the sunny Wednesday morning of her last week, Homer brought her out of the hospital in an ambulance and rolled her over on a stretcher to the gravesite to see everything. They sat and talked a long time while the ambulance crew waited.

A NEW VENTURE

Homer paid the crew for their time along with a nice tip. Homer even brought a thermos of Earl Grey tea, which he poured in Mama's favorite Swiss porcelain teacup, and he gave her a little bite of her favorite Auer chocolate from Geneva, Switzerland. Angelina loved things from Switzerland, although Homer never knew why. She savored the taste of the chocolate for several long moments while laying on her side on the stretcher. She looked at the mausoleum, smiling and told Homer she was so pleased and that he was the best thing she had ever created in life. The Earl Grey, she drank slowly. When the cup was empty, Angelina leaned up on her right arm and reached out to touch Homer's face. She looked into his eyes for a moment, her face serene and at peace. He remembered this as if it had just happened that morning. She looked at him, and then she said something he could never understand.

"Homer, you are him. I will always love you both." After she said the few words, she lay back down on the stretcher and closed her eyes. By the time the attendants rolled her back to the ambulance, the attendants noticed that Angelina had stopped breathing. Homer looked at them and was stern.

"No sirens, no flashing lights. And drive slowly back to the hospital. I will ride in the back, and when we get to the hospital, I will make sure you don't get in any trouble." Homer spoke softly but firmly.

"Yes, sir. We understand. We're sorry for your loss, Mr. Pitts."

"Thank you, boys. Thank you."

The ride seemed long but only lasted fifteen minutes. When they returned to the hospital, Homer arranged to take her to the morgue and then to the funeral home. Her ex-husband saw her at the funeral home along with his four boys. They were all a great deal older than Homer, but it was clear to everyone that Homer was in charge at the funeral home and for the funeral. He barely spoke to his father and stepbrothers. They were all alcoholics and in various stages of dying themselves. None of them would live more than a year after Angelina died, and Homer would bury each of them respectfully and efficiently. And in the ground. Only his mama had a mausoleum above ground. She was the grandest of all. These were the thoughts that constantly swirled through Homer's head when he went to the cemetery.

A few months after she died, Homer had a granite bench installed in the mausoleum to have a place to sit when he visited. On this visit, around lunchtime, there were a few other folks in the cemetery. But her mausoleum was in a distant corner, away from the other graves. So, as he spoke softly to his mother, no one else was around to interfere and listen.

"Mama, I'm doing pretty well. The Agapovs are wonderful, and the children are growing up fast. I had a man visit me from New York. Something financial, I think, but not quite sure what the interest is. And I got Main Street named after you and me. I miss you very much, my dear, and I wish you were here to see what your boy has been doing. But wherever you may be, I want you to know that I love you and think of you every day. I am running a little low on money these days and need to consider business pursuits. Please pray for me as I try to set up this new business."

He closed his eyes and sat quietly for a while, waiting on an answer.

"I don't have enough money to continue to support the Agapovs, run the estate, and help people in town, but I also think that those three

A NEW VENTURE

things help some mighty fine people. So, if I don't do it, I will be hurting those closest to me now. That would be selfish on my part, I think."

He let his words sink in so that her answer would be fully informed.

"But I also feel like I have worked very hard over the years and been blessed with resources sufficient to my needs. I have lived within my means and provided for others. To now risk it all on a business pursuit that is one of my wild dreams seems silly. Mama, I am perplexed as to what I should do. I await a sign to help me with this agonizing decision."

Homer sat for a few moments to see if a sign would materialize. He listened and looked around the cemetery, but nothing jumped out. A little bird flew over to the mausoleum, and Homer thought maybe there would be a sign. But the little bird's droppings on the windowsill ended that thought. Homer reached into his pocket and pulled out one of his monogrammed handkerchiefs. He always carried at least two when he came to visit Mama. He wiped the droppings off the granite windowsill. A sign was not forthcoming yet, but that's the way it was sometimes.

Homer always finished by reading the 23rd Psalm, which he also had inscribed in the mausoleum. The valley and the shadow of death. And still waters and comfort. It was his little ritual. He didn't go to church as he should anymore. Most Sundays, he convinced himself that he was too tired for church services, so he would sit on his patio and read a good piece in the New Yorker or the Sunday Times. But here in the cemetery at the mausoleum, he felt close to his mama and God. He felt like she was interceding for him to get the Holy Father's support. And Homer thought that they were both pulling for him while he was finding his way down here. Today, he needed to believe that that support was genuine as he thought about his challenges. And about the people of Grace. He kissed the porcelain portrait of his mama and then turned and walked toward his old Porsche sports car. And as he came closer to the vehicle, the sign came into focus, much to Homer's delight and bringing a broad grin to his face. He put on his sunglasses as he approached the car, with a little more pep in his step. The sign was unmistakable on a giant billboard right across from the cemetery—just one big, beautiful word on the billboard. A single word in red letters ten feet high gave Homer all the inspiration and guidance he needed: Biltmore.

CHAPTER 11

▲

BILTMORE

"Vladimir, Valentina!" Homer shouted with urgency just as the idea popped into his head.

"Prepare, my good people, for a road trip," he announced as they came running to see what he needed.

"Where?" Vladimir called out.

"Asheville, North Carolina. A one-day expedition to a place you have never been. A trip to explore our future."

"Splendid, Mister Homer. I will pack our lunches," Valentina said.

"No, No, Valentina. Just some drinks and snacks. We will enjoy lunch there. It's part of the discovery we need to do together."

"Okay!" Valentina would have a day off, it appeared. She was excited. "Is there somewhere specific we are going in this Asheville, North Carolina?"

"Oh, most definitely, my dear. The grandest, largest home in America. Modeled on a French chateau and estate. It is an epiphany for our estate's future."

"Does the magical kingdom have a name, Mister Homer?" Vladimir was curious now.

"Da. One word. Biltmore."

"Ah, you mean like they built more than anyone else?" Vladimir tried to understand the derivation. He did better with English when he understood where the words came from.

"Well, you could say that, and that is a nice assessment, Vladimir. But the estate was built by a man named George Vanderbilt, and the name came from his name."

"Oh," Valentina chimed in.

"The trip will take us about four hours, and we will go through the mountains. Let's plan to leave no later than 6 a.m. That will get us there by late morning. We can have an early lunch and do our inspection in the afternoon. Each of us will have a specific assignment, and I will hand those out this evening." Homer was on a mission now, and he wanted to learn what was required to transform his estate into a moneymaker. He felt sure that he could make this work and save the estate and the Agapovs from possible financial ruin with proximity to Atlanta. But he also needed to think about how to fold in the budding tennis stars he envisioned. It would have to be more than just a Biltmore look-alike. The eventual estate should be a thriving manor with athletes and celebrities in mind. And fashion shows. He thought that would be a nice touch that didn't exist anywhere in the South. His mind was working overtime now, so he retired to his study to plot out the empire he was about to build. And fate was conspiring to give him a little nudge and some needed publicity half a world away.

The Biltmore Estate comprises 8,000 acres in a beautiful mountain valley with a 250-room mansion and 175,000 square feet, a dairy, a winery, vineyard, two hotels, formal gardens, and ponds on the

BILTMORE

banks of the French Broad River. From the indoor swimming pool to the massive banquet hall, it was magnificent—and expensive to maintain. The wealthy family who owned it eventually turned it into a business to be to afford its upkeep. And now, it would need to be the model for Homer, so he could keep what he had built. He would create a tourist attraction for Grace like Biltmore was for Asheville. But Homer had to face some realities. His home didn't have a name, but that could be remedied. And he only had twelve rooms in 6500 square feet on 300 acres. Substantially smaller all around, but Homer thought there were also some advantages. Grace was a short drive from Atlanta, a major city with the busiest airport in the country. The mountains were not far, but there was no need to drive through the mountains to get to his estate. And if he could get Alvin's help, Homer was already considering a broader offering at his estate that included sports and athletics. He needed to identify something historical about the place, and it was clear that there would need to be some additional buildings.

A name. What could he call his estate? It needed to be short, memorable, catchy, upscale, and something that would serve as a brand. Maybe on the trip the next day they could do it together. Valentina and Vladimir, and the kids, might have good ideas.

The house started stirring early, around 5:30 a.m. The idea was to get out by 6:00 a.m. and arrive by 10. Vladimir had the car ready, gassed up, loaded up, and warmed up. The air was cool, but it would be pretty warm by noon, even in the mountains around Asheville. Valentina made some Russian blinis and sliced fruit to take along. A case of bottled water and a twelve-pack of colas rode along as well.

Vladimir and Mikhail shared driving responsibilities. Homer had a supply of orange juice, cranberry juice, bourbons, and Russian Standard vodka. But that would be for later in the day. Homer walked quickly out to the car with enthusiasm and his mug of chocolate pecan latte, specially made by Valentina. The kids limped out to the car, complaining that they shouldn't have to get up so early during spring break. They had blankets and pillows and intended to use the driving time to take naps. Mikhail sat in the front with Papa, who would be taking the first shift of driving. Valentina sat just behind Papa. Homer's reading materials included the previous Sunday's New York Times, last month's New Yorker, and some local flavor with the current magazine of Atlanta. The entourage pulled away at 6:07 AM. Not bad for a weekday during spring break.

The first phase of the trip was through the North Georgia mountains—an hour on a two-lane road in gently rolling hills. The elevation was still less than two thousand feet, and the driving was pretty quick. They passed through the towns of Ellijay and Blue Ridge, and then it was only about twenty miles to the North Carolina state line. In North Carolina, they rolled through a valley toward Murphy before things slowed down when they entered the Nantahala National Forest. The roads were curving and the elevation heightening with beautiful, scenic, forested mountains all around. And as they rolled forward, the younger kids slept, Valentina dozed, Vladimir and Mikhail talked about Russian forests and bears and Papa's experiences as an engineer and very little about his time in the Russian army. Homer finished his readings and fixed a cocktail of orange juice, cranberry juice, and green tea with hibiscus. It was his unique concoction for long trips and bladder and prostate health. He thought about trademarking it once but shelved the idea as too intrusive and personal. On the other hand, he might revisit it and market the combination under his yet-to-be-decided estate trademark.

"Vladimir and Valentina, I have a task for you. More like a riddle. The kids are welcome to contribute. We need to name our estate. Like Biltmore, but something snazzier. What ideas can any of you venture forth?"

"Homerbilt?" Valentina said. It was her first thought, done while also knitting some socks for her not-yet-conceived grandchildren.

"It has merit," Homer said in a supportive way.

"Homer's Castle," Mikhail offered.

"Okay."

"Homerton Abbey," Tanya offered. She was a devoted fan of a television show about an English manor with "abbey" in the name.

"Nice," Homer answered.

"The Bard's Gardens," Sonya said in her soft-spoken way. Sonya was a quiet girl. Peaceful, with a transcendent spirit. Almost always smiling, and when not, her face was filled with empathy for all those around her. She loved the world and all that was in it. The plants, the animals. She loved walking with Mikhail through the woods. She would spend hours playing by the little creek that ran through the estate. She could see, almost with a sixth sense, into the heart of things.

Homer contemplated her contribution but did not say anything. He looked out the window of his car into the passing green and purple mountains. Alive with the spirit of the world and yet mysterious in the shadows.

"The Bard's Gardens," he said wistfully. "Sonya, you have won the contest! For this, you will get the finest dessert of your choice when we have lunch at the Biltmore." A cheer went up from all the Agapovs. Homer as well. Sonya blushed. She was humble, and the thought had been blurted out as soon as it came into her precious mind, without a moment of calculation or pridefulness. She had been reading about the ancient Homer of Greek tradition. The Iliad and Odyssey but also that he was a blind bard traveling the countryside. And Mr. Homer was not blind, but he was a bit of a bard, she thought. It all just fit together, and you shouldn't name everything in town after Mr. Homer. It would overuse his name and make it a point of ridicule and jokes. No, she thought that the estate should be named somehow while preserving the connection to Mr. Homer. So, that's how she had created a name—The Bard's Garden.

The morning was warming up, and the entourage was closing in on their destination as they passed Lake Junaluska with just twenty more miles to go. And then, suddenly, the dreaded scream.

"Bathroom. Got to go!" exclaimed Sasha. Little Sasha was quiet during the whole trip, and there had been no urgent stops. Now the urgency was palpable.

"Got to go. Got to go." Sasha exclaimed again. Valentina tried to calm Sasha down, Vladimir grabbed his forehead, and Mikhail, who had just taken over the driving duties, began to sweat. They were in the roadside bathroom dead zone—no bathrooms for at least five miles. In the everyday world, five miles was probably less than ten minutes. But, in the extraordinary world of the long-distance trip, the five miles seemed to go on forever. And there were waves of urgency for poor Sasha. Like waves at the beach. Building, building, reaching a crest and then crashing with a scream and a whimper, and "I have to gos," and then the moment would pass as the next wave began. Five miles, five cycles. Finally, a two-pump gas station came into view with a sign for restrooms. Mikhail whipped the limo into the gas station and pulled around to the side. Sasha jumped out along with Valentina, and they rushed up to the bathroom door. Sasha grabbed the door and turned the knob. Except that it didn't turn. It was locked. Valentina tried. No different. They turned and looked at Mikhail and Vladimir with panic on their faces. Mikhail jumped from the limo driver's seat and bounded toward the entrance of the store. He rushed in with urgency.

"Sir, Sir, we need to open the bathroom."

"You need the key."

"Yes, please, the key."

"Got to buy something first. For most folks, that would be gas." The voice from behind the counter came from a skeletal-looking man with a long gray beard, a sunburn, a prematurely-aged beak of a nose, scaly face, metal-framed sunglasses, and cowboy hat. He leaned back, sitting on his stool, and held a cigar to his lips.

"Okay, here! I will buy this." Mikhail held up a candy bar with a wrapper that read "Millionaire Surprise!" The label said that it was dark chocolate wrapping a soft caramel center with peanuts. The wrapper felt old, as if the bar may have been sitting on the counter for years.

"That will be $5.99 plus tax," the ancient man said, seemingly without moving his mouth at all.

"But the package says 99 cents?" Vladimir, who now joined

Mikhail, boomed out.

"It's $5.99 plus tax," the man replied.

"Okay. Here are six dollars."

"Sales tax adds 42 cents. So that is $6.41."

Mikhail looked at the man, incredulous at this delay. He reached into his pocket and pulled out 40 cents.

"Here, 40 cents more," Mikhail exclaimed.

"Short one cent," the man replied.

"Give us the key. We have to go. My daughter has to go!" Vladimir angrily yelled.

"Sorry. One cent more." The man wouldn't budge.

Vladimir was beside himself now, but the man behind the counter was actually in a four-foot square box made out of two-inch-thick bulletproof glass. There was no way to get in. So, the man behind the counter was holding all the cards for now. Mikhail pulled out his wallet, pulled out his emergency $20, and pushed it under the window. The man seemed satisfied and took the twenty. He moved the six he already had back under the window where the forty cents was still sitting. He reached over to the cash register and put in the twenty. Then he pulled out ten and two ones.

"I'm a couple of dollars short. I need to go in the back to the safe to get some ones. Be right back."

The man disappeared into an unseen door before Mikhail or Vladimir could say anything. A few minutes went by as both Mikhail and Vladimir were now sweating. The gas station man finally came back and pushed the change under the window. And then the key. An old brass key with a board tied to it. Mikhail took the key and ran.

BILTMORE

Vladimir picked up the change.

"Here you go, Mama." Mikhail handed the key to Valentina, who took the key in her trembling hands as Sasha sobbed. The door unlocked, and the two rushed in. Maybe too quickly because the stench from the unflushed toilet propelled them back out of the bathroom, off their feet, sort of like an unseen monster.

"Oh my!" Valentina exclaimed.

Quick-thinking, Mikhail dove into the bathroom and flushed the toilet. A can of freshener was on the sink, so he sprayed as he backed out of the restroom from hell. Once he was safely back outside, Mikhail sprayed the jet of tropical scented spray into the bathroom. He emptied the nearly full can. Finally, Sasha could enter. Mama wiped the seat, and Sasha relieved herself. And relieved herself. And relieved herself. When poor little Sasha finished doing her business, she had probably lost half her body weight. One urgency then replaced another.

"I am hungry and thirsty!" she exclaimed. This could wait the fifteen minutes it would take to make it to the Biltmore estate. A couple of the other kids held their noses and entered the prehistoric bathroom. Mikhail returned the key and purchased eight more Millionaire candy bars for the other kids. Sasha finished hers in three bites and received the second one for being a good sport. She thought they were the best candy bars she had ever eaten.

Homer remained detached from the bathroom drama as he finished the final story in the New Yorker. A little piece entitled "*A Swiss Count Comes Clean: Count St. Clare and his New York Daze.*" It was a review of a small book written by a reclusive billionaire in Geneva who spent formative years in his father's multinational company's Manhattan branch. Reading the review, Homer felt a kinship with the man that he could not explain.

The Agapov-Pitts clan rolled into the Biltmore front gate at 11:15 am. Twelve tickets to enter were presented, and then they moved through and began the trek toward the mansion. A slightly winding road passed a river on the right as they drove. Then open fields interspersed with forests emerged. They passed a hotel but kept going, climbing up a small hill until they saw it. Homer could hear oohs and ahs from the Agapovs, and Mikhail worked hard to stay focused on driving. Then they rounded a bend, and a full view of the home came into focus. Mikhail parked the limo occupying two spaces at the far end of the parking lot. Everyone piled out of the car, and the merry band made their way toward the house.

Reaching the front entrance, they went into the banquet hall, massive with its organ. And on and on. When they initially entered the giant home, no one was starving, so they spent the next hour walking through it until Sasha announced that she was "famished," a new word she learned that past week at school before Spring Break. Then the group headed to the restaurant for lunch. While the entourage ate, Homer slipped away to a previously scheduled, private meeting with the general manager of Biltmore for a candid discussion on what it would take to have a working estate. Homer returned just in time for dessert and coffee. He was sobered by the discussion but also optimistic that he could pull it off. Diversification would be essential, and the idea of an athletic component resonated with the manager with whom he met.

BILTMORE

"Well, what do you think?" Homer asked the Agapovs.

"Oh, Mr. Homer, it's beautiful!" Valentina gushed.

"Lots of upkeep, if you ask me." Vladimir was pragmatic because he knew that he would have to do much of the work himself if they were to replicate in Grace a Biltmore-like estate.

"I would like to be a butler in such a fine home," Mikhail said, working on his English accent with the belief that it would enhance his chances of becoming a first-class butler.

"I like the toy store. Can I have a toy to take home?" Sasha said.

Everyone had different opinions, but all were glowingly positive.

Homer then asked a fundamental question to which he received a unanimous if delayed, response.

"Do you think we can do something like Biltmore with our estate?" he smiled at Sasha, and she sweetly smiled back.

The Agapovs looked at each other. And then all the family looked at Vladimir.

"Da! Yes, we can do it!" he said confidently, and everyone cheered. They would give it their best effort. And Vladimir stood up with his vanilla cream soda and raised it to toast Mr. Homer.

"Mister Homer, you are special, and we love you. We thank you, and yes, we will help you build the estate!" and all the Agapovs raised their glasses to toast.

"And, let me toast you." Homer stood and raised his glass to the Agapovs in the spirit of the Russian tradition of mealtime toasts. "To the best people I know. May your lives be long and prosperous and filled with love!" The family left the restaurant and went to their assignments. Anya, Tanya, Masha, Ekaterina, Sonya, Sasha, and Ludmilla went with

Valentina to tour the gardens. Beautiful roses in the extensive Rose garden. Bromeliads in the Conservatory, and a wide variety of flowers in the Walled Garden. They marveled at all the types and the beauty. Mikhail and Boris joined Vladimir and rode a shuttle to Deerpark to see the horse riding and carriage operation.

At 3 p.m., the Biltmore manager arranged for the family to see the dairy, and at 4 p.m., the winery. At 5 p.m., the day ended as the family loaded back into the car and headed out. Before they left, they stopped at the store to buy Sasha a toy and snacks for the drive. The drive was long, and half of it was in the dark. Mikhail drove first, in the daylight, and then Vladimir took over as it got darker. The children and Valentina dozed off. But Homer kept working at his little impromptu desk in the rear seat. Homer moved numbers around and added and subtracted all over, again and again. He finally figured out how to get to the stage of having an estate that broke even. Getting to a profit would be more difficult. He was melancholy as he tried to make the numbers work. But he couldn't see a way forward. He flipped off the light on his little impromptu desk and looked out the window filled with ambivalence and angst. To do what he wanted would take some luck and maybe a minor miracle.

CHAPTER 12

NEW PURSUITS

Homer and the Agapovs finally pulled into the estate around 10:30 p.m. There were no stops on the way back, but as soon as they rolled in, the race was on to get to one of the four bathrooms—three waves of flushes for each bathroom. Homer went to his study and put his notes away. But he still couldn't put away his thoughts. He loved what he had seen at Biltmore, and he wanted to create something unique that folks around town would be proud of for years to come—something beautiful and stately and impressive. And since he had no family left, he fully intended to leave everything to the Agapovs, even though he had not told them that yet. But whatever gifts or inheritance for them he would give would have to be self-sufficient and sustainable. And for that to happen, he needed to build more, which made no sense since Homer was already facing financial challenges. It wasn't pragmatic to dream up a new enterprise, but Homer's grandiosity and dreams were as much a part of him as his myopic eyes and bald head. And once he started one of his fantastical projects, he wouldn't let it go.

Homer thought the Bard's Garden was a great name, but it wouldn't work for the entire estate. He needed something more ancient, something that immediately implied mystery and dynasty. His estate would be more than a home. It would require a castle, and the castle had to hearken back to medieval times, an origin that connected Homer's estate to European mystery. He wasn't sure why he was drawn to these ideas or how they would take shape, but he felt this was the path.

The current home was a family home, not a grand showpiece like what they had seen at Biltmore. Homer's castle would have to be extravagant, and for that, he needed to acquire more land. A lot more land. At least a thousand acres for the estate. He knew of three properties adjoining his that might be sold to him, and with those lands, he would have more than a thousand acres.

The old Longfellow farm had been sitting fallow for a decade. Carl and Lula Bell wanted to sell but waited for the land to appreciate before they would let it go. They had been told to break it up to get more money. If Homer was going to convince them to sell it as one parcel, he couldn't skimp on them. Their five hundred acres sat next door to Homer's current estate, and there were two other parcels with a little over two hundred acres apiece. A real castle would be at least four stories, stone walls, moat, drawbridge. To buy the land and build the castle would consume all of his money and more. Without new income coming in, he would go bankrupt and lose everything he had. He would need Alvin's help to build a self-sustaining castle estate, to turn a wild dream into a reality. Alvin was a terrific businessman, and he had the discipline to make this work. As sleep was falling over Homer, the name for the castle finally emerged in his thoughts. Castle Gratia, grace in Latin. It was starting to come together as a vision: the Bard's Gardens would surround Castle Gratia.

NEW PURSUITS

The next day, as the Agapovs and Homer were having a lazy morning and late morning brunch, still recovering from their one-day expedition, down at the town square, two men were meeting for an early lunch to explore a new opportunity.

"Major Lowman, thank you for meeting me for lunch," former Sheriff Meeks said.

"You're welcome. What can I do for you?" Lowman said as he took a bite of his Double Cheeseburger with cheddar cheese, tomato, onion, slaw, and bacon—the signature burger at the Back Street Burger Shack. Lowman loved the burger, so he had two instead of French fries, onion rings, or a salad.

"Major Lowman, I have retired as sheriff, or more accurately, have been fired," Meeks confessed. "It all stems from my little accident at the celebration at Homer Pitts' house. I will get a pension and benefits, but I leave the department with my reputation besmirched. I need to change that and am looking for a way to rehabilitate my reputation. I have always loved history and would relish, under these circumstances, the opportunity to delve into local history. So, I was thinking, what about being an assistant to you, an assistant town historian? I could work with you for free."

Lowman looked at former Sheriff Meeks for a moment squinting his eyes and considering the possibilities.

"Well, what are your qualifications?"

"I have over thirty years in the town's sheriff's department. Before that, I was a street cop in Atlanta. I have an associate degree in criminal justice. I have lived in Grace most of my life, went to Grace High School where I played tennis and golf and was in charge of the yearbook, and

I was a senior fundraiser."

Major Lowman listened closely. He took a big bite of his second burger and chewed it slowly until he swallowed the mush. Then he finally spoke.

"Terrific. Those are some good qualifications. How about you join me on a trial basis, and we will see where it goes from there?"

Meeks was ecstatic.

"Sounds exciting. When can I start?"

"You already started as far as I am concerned."

"Tickled. I am just tickled."

The two middle-aged, well-meaning men finished their lunch. They then walked around the downtown area, eventually making it to the Grace History Museum, a one-room storefront on the square across Homer Pitts Avenue. They spent the rest of the afternoon going over the exhibits and getting former Sheriff Meeks up to speed on the priorities and activities of the History Museum. Those conversations only took about fifteen minutes. They spent most of their time together gossiping and talking about sports.

CHAPTER 13

▲

THE STORY ABOUT THE SWISS MAN

New York Lights magazine was a favorite of Homer's. He contributed several articles over the years, and they paid well. He also liked the lifestyle stories that other authors wrote. An article caught Homer's eye, but not just for its literary quality.

"Count Armand St. Clare remains an icon of restrained style even as he approaches his eighty-seventh year. Outfitted with a classic Brioni suit complemented by silk scarf and tortoiseshell sunglasses, the diminutive Count was exuberant when we interviewed him in fading late afternoon light on the terrace of his estate by Lake Geneva." The piece wasn't long but was beautifully written and informative. The story described how the Count a couple of years in New York learning the inner workings of his father's business empire, an empire he would later inherit. The only child of an only child, the Count shared that he now lived a solitary life. He had friends, business associates, and distant relatives. But after his mother and father passed on, unmarried and without a child, he was the only one person left to remember the intimate moments of his life. Family dinners, Zermatt, Lake Como, Monaco, and Nice, and his first trip to see New York City with his father. His parents lived to be old, but he still had been without them now for the last thirty years. He missed them, told the interviewer, and felt the sunset coming on his family line. The interviewer began to probe into the Count's love life over the years and even during his time in New York. But the Count redirected, swiftly and delicately moving on to other topics, sidestepping the discussion. He liked to talk about his beautiful home by Lake Geneva or his 45-hectare working farm in the valley near the French border, with a 400-year-old house, gardens, and vineyards. Or his art collection or his charitable foundation. The interviewer accommodated the Count, and they moved on to the other topics. At least for what made it to print.

In London, Archie dealt with two issues from the Count's past that didn't appear in the article. The tests and the people.

"The tests are inconclusive. We hoped to do some rapid tests on a few loci, but that didn't work. We probably don't have enough DNA in the sample we got," the lab director from New York said on a phone call to the Captain and Archie as they sat in Archie's London office.

"Another sample then?" the Captain asked.

"Well, really, we need a sample from the mother, but from what I understand, so that would be challenging. Any chance we could get a sample from her?" the lab director responded.

"Not sure. We are doing this quietly. I will talk with the Count." Archie responded and hung up.

Both the Captain and Archie knew that a sample from the mother would not be possible. At least at this moment, there was no reasonable way to obtain the sample.

"When is your flight back to New York?" Archie asked the Captain.

THE STORY ABOUT THE SWISS MAN

▲

"A little after six," the Captain responded.

"It's already four, so you better get going. Thank you for coming over to the pond and debriefing with us in person. I think the additional details about your visit helped get a complete picture for the Count." Archie said.

"I enjoyed myself while I was here," the Captain said with a slight smile without divulging his side activities the night before.

"Good. I will contact Mr. Pitts and set up the trip for him. You should plan to be in Switzerland when he comes so that he has at least one familiar face around."

"Right-O," the Captain got up, shook hands, and disappeared out the door.

Archie was left pondering the next steps. The lab would finish up with what they had and get him a final report in the next couple of days. The issue of maternal DNA was delicate, and he would need to thoroughly brief the Count before he brought it up. And the time-sensitive conclusion of the investigation and any actions to be taken were foremost on Archie's mind. The Count was seemingly healthy right now, but he didn't need to be sick to die suddenly at almost ninety. Old age could cause that—any issues about inheritances or succession at the company required expeditious resolution. Archie wasn't sure that this little exercise in Georgia would amount to anything, but leaving the future in limbo too long made Archie quite uncomfortable.

CHAPTER 14

ALVIN, I HAVE ANOTHER PROPOSITION

Alvin was returning from his six-mile morning run when Homer called.

"Homer, it's early," Alvin said between huffs on his final sprint.

"Alvin, I want to build a castle, and I need your help."

"Homer, I don't build castles," Alvin exclaimed as he finished the run.

"But you are an expert businessman, right?" Homer continued.

"Yes," Alvin said.

"So, I need an expert businessman to help me craft a business plan that will help me become a successful castle builder." Homer made it sound somewhat logical.

"Why?" Alvin said.

"Legacy," Homer said.

"Vanity," Alvin responded.

"Town legacy, not my legacy," Homer clarified.

"Still, smells like vanity to me. Does the town want a castle?"

"Yes, but they don't know it yet."

"When do you plan on telling them?"

"When we craft a business plan to build it," Homer responded.

"What's with us?" Alvin asked.

"You're the businessman, and I am the dreamer," Homer stated.

"But I didn't agree to this yet."

"But you will," Homer said.

"How do you know that?"

"Third grade, recess, basketball court. You told me that you would be rich one day. And I said you would become the world's most financially successful athlete. I told you how and what to do. You trusted me, did what I said, and now you are," Homer recounted.

"I am what?"

"The world's most financially successful athlete!"

"Not there yet. Maybe never be there."

"But you are a lot further along the road to that goal than when you started."

"Yes, I can't disagree. But how does that relate to this castle nonsense?" Alvin asked.

"Castle Gratia and Bard's Gardens will be an illustrious medieval estate in the foothills of Georgia. A place of honor, of peace, of solitude, of grace, in Grace, by the people of Grace." Homer's description sounded like an advertisement for a time-share.

"Sounds corny."

"Well, we still need a business plan," Homer repeated.

"Okay."

"Okay, what?"

"Okay, I am in," Alvin relented. "Do I have to pay for anything?"

"Let's figure out a way to fund it without you paying anything or at least making sure you get an outstanding return on any investment. It shouldn't be built on charity because it won't last. It needs a good business plan. That's your contribution," Homer said with an eye toward Alvin's long-term engagement.

"Sounds good to me. Okay, when do we start?" Alvin said.

"Tomorrow at 9 a.m. How about we meet at Café Latte in the square. You know Henry's little place," Homer responded.

"Okay, is Henry part of this?"

"He might be but doesn't know it yet."

"Okay. See you tomorrow, nine at Henry's. What about the tennis courts and lessons?" Alvin asked.

"Vladimir starts building today," Homer responded.

"Lessons in two weeks then. And I need to evaluate those girls this week just to make sure they can do it."

"Okay. I will give you an update tomorrow."

Earlier in the morning, unbeknownst to Homer or the rest of the sleeping Agapovs, Vladimir and Mikhail had begun work on the tennis courts. For three tennis courts, about one-fourth of an acre needed clearing, which they did by lunch. After lunch, they planned to go to the building supply store to get supplies to complete the courts based on Vladimir's perusal of how-to videos on his iPhone.

"Nice progress, Vladimir." Homer was pleased as lunch approached. Vladimir, sweating and shirtless with the May sun beating down on him, walked to Homer to talk.

"Thank you, Mr. Homer. We will go to the store after lunch to pick up the supplies to build the surface. We also need to rent a truck and get the fence materials."

"Okay. Have the charges put on my account."

"Yes. Mr. Homer. The courts will be expensive to build. Does your account have a limit high enough for all the expenses, or does it need to be increased?"

"How much?"

"I figure about $25,000 per court. $75,000 total."

Homer gulped. He hadn't counted on the courts costing that much, but he knew Vladimir would give him an accurate assessment and build them to perfection. Homer had the money, and the credit wouldn't be a problem. But he also knew that these kinds of projects would eat up his capital quickly.

"Okay. Let's go forward. I will call the store and increase the credit line."

Homer needed Alvin to do the girls' assessments right away. If a couple of the girls weren't going to have tennis in their future, they might be able to eliminate building one of the courts. But if they all could do it, he wanted each girl to have an equal opportunity.

Homer went back inside the house and sat in the large kitchen with Valentina and Sasha. Sasha was helping her mama peel potatoes for lunch. Homer pitched in as he sat at the rectangular wooden table that occupied the center of the kitchen. Counters and cabinets lined the walls of the kitchen. A bay window over the sink gave the three of them a beautiful view out into the pasture and the woods beyond.

"Sasha, did you enjoy our little trip to Biltmore yesterday?"

"Why, of course, Mr. Homer. I loved everything about our future home."

Homer swallowed hard. "Our future home?"

"Oh yes, I believe I will have my own bedroom, maybe on the third floor. The blue room. That was my favorite at the Biltmore Mansion."

"Now, Sasha, where did you get the idea that we are moving to Biltmore?"

"Oh, Mr. Homer, I didn't mean we are moving. But I see that Papa and Mikhail have started digging the ground to build a Biltmore here. Right out there." She turned and pointed at the bay window toward the pasture and the area Vladimir and Mikhail were clearing.

"My little dear, I don't know what to say. I am not sure we are going to be a replica of Biltmore here. There is only one, but we can learn from it. But what about a castle?"

"A castle. Oh yes. I like that idea. Will it be a big castle?"

"Yes, I think so. But I have to work out the details."

"Can my room be in a tower?"

"You want to be in the tower? Like a prisoner?"

"No, not a prisoner but like a princess!" Sasha corrected Homer.

"Okay, then that's what we will do!"

"A castle, you say, Mister Homer?" Valentina asked.

"Yes, Valentina, a castle. I thought about it last night when we got back. I ran it over and over in my mind and concluded that a castle is the only thing that makes it worth doing."

"Mr. Homer, has anyone built a castle here? Do we have Mongols running from the forest to pillage us?" Valentina asked, invoking a little of the Russian historical experience.

"Ah, no, Valentina. We don't have Mongols running from the forest to pillage us."

"Do we have Lithuanians or Swedes or Poles or Ottomans or French invading us? Are the Cossacks rebelling? Are German tanks rolling?" Valentina asked with a sincere expression.

"No, my dear Valentina. No, we don't have anybody invading."

"Then why do we need a castle?" Valentina asked innocently.

"Because I think it would be special and would bring visitors."

"Visitors? To our estate? Oh, like Biltmore. I see now. And we would have something different, right?" Valentina responded as she began to understand Homer's strategy.

"That's the idea."

"How big does it have to be to be a castle?"

"Very big," Homer answered curtly. He could elaborate on the specifics that he had been reviewing over and over. But he didn't think Valentina needed all that.

"Will we live there or work there?" she inquired.

"Work for sure and maybe live too," Homer responded, not sure.

"Okay," Valentina answered.

"Now, what's for lunch with these potatoes we are peeling?" Homer asked.

"A nice, big roasted chicken. It's about to come out of the oven," Valentina said as she got up and opened the oven door.

"Oh, yes, I can smell it now. Yum, yum."

Homer was hungry but thought of something he needed to do before lunch. He left the kitchen and went to his library. He had several books on castles. A pet interest of his as a kid, Homer had several large books with pictures of castles. Books with photos and descriptions of castles from Germany, France, Britain, Scandinavia, Italy, and Switzerland. He thumbed through them until he found the page he remembered. The detailed plans he remembered from his

ALVIN, I HAVE ANOTHER PROPOSITION

▲

childhood were from a book published in 1958 that his mother gave him. He found the chapter on castles in Switzerland. He remembered that he liked the Aigle Castle. Aigle was an excellent place to start, and it would fit on the land he already had. Maybe an additional land acquisition could come later, and he might even enlarge the castle. He just needed an architect to update the plans a bit and accommodate for future growth.

Homer rarely ate lunch during the week, much less a big meal with the Agapovs. Today, he was eating with them and helped Valentina prepare the meal. Along with the roast chicken, she made ground beef and pork meatballs she called "her Siberian cutlets," along with potatoes, cucumber-tomato salad with dill and onion, baked bread, pickles, and a host of sweets for later, along with hot tea from the samovar. Vladimir and Mikhail moved the large kitchen table outside under the big oak tree in sight of the bay window. They covered the table with a white tablecloth and put juice and ice water out along with the plates, silverware, and napkins. The food came out with each one of the kids carrying a dish.

"Mr. Homer, will you say the blessing?" Vladimir asked. As everyone sat down, Homer knew that the Agapovs usually said an Orthodox prayer that was quite lengthy and included the Lord's Prayer, which he forgot about thirty years ago. He didn't have a prayer book to read from, so he had to wing it from the heart.

"Oh Lord, we thank you for our food that nourishes our bodies and for your love for us. Bless this food and our day that it is filled with love, peace, and grace. Amen"

"Amen" was repeated by all the Agapovs, forcefully—all eleven voices. And then they sat down and started to eat. The meal went on with storytelling and second helpings. The air was warm but not too hot. The sun was filtered by the branches of the oak tree, with new spring leaves. A slight breeze kept everything fresh. After the main dishes, Valentina, with help from everyone, cleared the table and brought the dishes inside, starting the full dishwasher. Vladimir and Mikhail teamed up to carry the large samovar outside for tea, placing it in the middle of the long table. They laughed and sang some Russian folk songs. Homer even got up and danced to their singing with a little awkward shuffle he created on the spot. Like a bit of an elf, he was grinning and laughing and enjoying it all. And then the beautiful lunch ended. Homer thanked the Agapovs and headed to his office. Vladimir and Mikhail headed to the building supply store. The kids went back to enjoying their time off from school. And Valentina sat down for an hour of her favorite soap opera and a little light dozing in front of the television.

"Vladimir, you don't want to build a clay court," Jack Lincoln, the building supply store clerk, said. "Too much upkeep. You have to repaint the lines all the time, and it takes too long to dry. My eldest daughter was the Georgia state tennis champion back in her day, so I have seen all kinds of surfaces. I think you want concrete with a synthetic sealer. I can sell you the concrete, but you need to get the sealer from Atlanta. Now, how big is your court going to be?"

An engineer by training, Vladimir might have taken offense from being told by a semi-retired store clerk exactly how to build something. From anyone but Jack. Jack always gave good advice, and Vladimir liked Jack.

"How deep does the concrete need to be?" Vladimir asked.

"Four inches minimum, but I would probably go five inches. It adds twenty-five percent to the work and cost, but it's worth it." Jack said from experience.

"Okay, I need 3,845 cubic feet," Vladimir said.

"That's going to be $16,000, and you are going to need a truck to come out and pour it. Otherwise, it will take you way too long doing it bag by bag."

"Jack, have you ever built a tennis court?" Vladimir asked.

"For my daughter when she was growing up. We sold that house about twenty years ago. They tore up what was still an excellent tennis court to put in a pool. Go figure. But I built it all myself."

"Jack, what time you get off?" Vladimir asked.

"Well, Vladimir, at around 3 o'clock. Why?"

"I want you to come out to Mr. Homer's estate tomorrow and show me how to build these courts. I need an expert coaching me," Vladimir said.

"Okay. How about I come out around 3:30?"

"Yes. And you stay for dinner too. My Valentina will be cooking chicken, I think. Or maybe salmon."

Jack's wife died a couple of years back, and his kids all moved away years ago. He moved into a small house, really about the size of an apartment, and had a pretty simple life. Heading out to the estate sounded like an adventure worth the effort, so he was excited.

"Okay. I would enjoy that. Sounds good," Jack responded.

As Vladimir and Mikhail were driving back to the estate, Mikhail asked his father a tricky question he had been contemplating.

"Papa, when I come back from London, I will be your boss, right?"

"Son, what you have told me about the butler means that yes, I think you will be my boss."

"How will that work?"

"Fire me. Day one, you just fire me," Vladimir said.

"What?" Mikhail was confused.

"Yes. You have to. See, you don't know if you want an employee like me, and I don't know if I want a boss like you. So, you fire me, and then you either need me or not. If you do, then we negotiate. If you don't, then Mama and I and the kids move somewhere else."

For several minutes, there was a silence that was piercing in its totality: no music, no humming, no small talk. Just the sound of the truck tires rolling on an asphalt country road. Finally, Mikhail spoke.

"Well, I don't think Mr. Homer would let me fire you."

"Then you shouldn't work for him. You should work for a boss who will listen to you and let you run the estate like you think it should be run. If you don't, then you will be fired when something goes wrong, even if it's because of someone else's mistakes."

"Give me an example."

"Okay. You go to work for Mr. Homer, and you are his head butler. He tells me to build a tennis court with clay. I don't. I build it with concrete. And then Mr. Homer comes out and gets angry with me and wants me fired. But, I am your papa, and you don't want to fire me. So, Mr. Homer fires who? You!" Vladimir explained.

"Okay," Mikhail answered softly, the realization sinking in that the business world was pretty ruthless.

"But, if you and Mr. Homer agree that you are in charge and make

ALVIN, I HAVE ANOTHER PROPOSITION

the decisions, then you either fire me, or you don't, but it's your decision, not his. His decision is whether to put you in command or not. But your decisions are the ones that happen every day. The only way to do it."

"I get it. But if Mr. Homer will pay for everything, then I have to work for him, right?"

"That's between you and him. You have to have an agreement with him before you go for the training. Otherwise, you don't know what you owe him. This is about business and working, not about the family."

"Do you and Mama have an agreement with him?"

"Yes. He insisted that we have this agreement before we came. He said it was to protect us, and he was right. We know what he expects. That's how we get along so good, like family. So, you have to have an agreement with him too."

"Okay. But how do I set up this agreement?" Mikhail asked.

"Lawyer. You should go to Mr. Carl Longfellow. He is retired but still a good lawyer. And he has known Mr. Homer for many years."

"How do I do that?"

"You call him. Set up a time to go to see him. His wife, Lula Bell, will serve tea on the front porch of their house," Vladimir said.

"Okay, Papa. But I can't fire you," Mikhail said innocently.

"Then you should not be the butler here!"

Mikhail, for the first time, felt the weight of his chosen profession. He always imagined that he had only had to worry about his behavior. But now, in talking with his papa, Mikhail realized that he would be responsible for much more. He would need to be well-trained and competent, but he would also need to be strict, consistent, thorough, and wise. Mikhail knew he could be all those things and more and was excited. He was also becoming more convinced that it would be necessary to spend more time in Europe, whether it was London or Moscow or Paris or the Alps, to ensure that he had enough training and experience to make hard decisions with confidence. That might take longer than the two months he had planned.

"Papa, maybe I should stay in Europe longer to get more experience."

"Maybe. Maybe not. I don't know, but you are right to ask the question. You have to come back here, especially here, with confidence. If you are not confident, you will not be successful."

"I understand. I am glad we had this conversation."

"Yes. Good conversation to have. Your grandpapa had this conversation with me when I was eighteen. Grandpapa told me that I would have to get out on my own to learn to be a man. I went into the Army. Was sent to Afghanistan. Terrible, what I saw. When I came back, I was not the same person. I was wiser and sadder. The world will not be fair to you, and you will suffer in your life. But, if you are smart and wise and make good decisions, you can make a good life."

Mikhail realized that he knew little about his father's time as a soldier because his father would never talk about it. This was the most he had ever said to Mikhail about that time. Mikhail took it as an opportunity to learn more.

"Papa, what was it like in Afghanistan?"

"The land was beautiful. Tall mountains with snow. Forests on the slopes of the mountains. River with clear cold water. It was a beautiful land. The people were hospitable. Until they weren't, then it was the most terrible. The local men would slip away into the mountains. They could hide and not be detected. When we would walk on patrol, at least one of us would not return. We were in constant fear of the mujahideen. Ghosts. They would slip into our midst and cut a throat or take a head—or worse. I learned there the fragile nature of life. I still dream of my death there."

Mikhail looked at this father. Mikhail saw the creases in his father's face, the scar on his neck, and the weariness in his eyes. A part of his soul stayed in that place and continued to suffer—a place of beauty and gruesome death. Mikhail was relieved that his life was not forcing him to be in such a place, but Mikhail also realized how naïve he was, how inexperienced. And wisdom could not develop or flourish in such a man. He decided that he would have to spend longer in Europe to be seasoned and tested. He didn't tell his father that this was what he decided, and he couldn't tell his mama, at least not right now. He thought that the visit to Mr. Carl needed to come first. He needed to understand how best to negotiate with Mr. Homer. Mr. Carl could teach him some of those skills, he thought. But he knew that leaving his family here would be difficult. He also knew that he needed his own money. Mikhail had saved money for several months to help pay for butler's school. All of these thoughts filled his mind as they pulled back into the parking area of the estate. So much to consider. Going to college seemed like a simple thing now compared to all of these other decisions.

CHAPTER 15

BREAKFAST AT THE CAFE

The following day, Homer sat down at the table in the café, waiting for Alvin. He drove himself to the café, wanting the freedom to stay as long as needed and then run some errands. Homer also wanted Vladimir and Mikhail to continue to make progress on the tennis courts. Mikhail would be leaving before too long, and he was a massive help to his father. Together, the two of them could do almost anything.

"Homer, good morning. Coffee?" Henry asked. Henry was a fifty-ish short guy who looked like a biker, with a lot of prison time. Many scary-looking tattoos, greased pepper-black hair pulled back in a ponytail, and a penchant for wearing sleeveless blue jean jackets and blue jean pants with a white T-shirt and leather cowboy boots. In reality, Henry finished the University of Georgia with an accounting degree. He worked at an Atlanta consulting firm until his marriage fell apart in his thirties, and he started searching for his authentic self. He ended up neither as a biker nor in prison but a one-bedroom apartment above his café.

"Why yes, with cream and sugar. Thank you, Henry."

Henry smiled and nodded. He was back in a moment with piping hot coffee with just the right amount of sugar and cream. It was natural cream, no milk or fake cream. He also left Homer two little Belgian chocolates.

"Henry, you always get my order exactly right before I even place it," Homer said, also noticing the added touch of his favorite chocolates.

"Aim to please my customer. Just like you taught me."

When Henry moved back to Grace from Atlanta, he wanted this building. He was still fresh from losing his midtown Atlanta coffee shop's lease when a national chain muscled in. Henry had the lease but no equity. After nearly two decades of building a local clientele, he was kicked out and replaced by the national chain that charged $2 more a cup, and his former customers didn't even complain. He learned a hard lesson that no matter how profitable a business was, you had to plan for when it was over. And you had to leave with more than just the memories. This time around, Henry wanted to own his building, and if someone tried to move him out, he would get something for all his efforts. Equity was an essential thing for Henry. When he returned to Grace, Homer loaned Henry the money to buy the building and get started again, and it was Homer who taught him how to keep his customers more than simply happy—how to keep them intensely loyal. Henry was good with numbers and learned that end of business in school. But it was Homer who taught Henry the finer points of customer service.

For Homer, these skills were hard lessons learned early in his New York days. In Henry, Homer invested both money and time. Now, the success of the café was a tribute to Homer's confidence in Henry.

Henry paid Homer the money-back years ago, but his gratitude for Homer's support was as fresh and never-ending as the day he sat with Homer at the only table in that yet-to-be-opened café. Henry was Homer's friend, and Homer was Henry's friend and a loyal customer as well. So, Henry was patiently listening to Homer's drawn-out explanation for what he wanted to do.

"Henry, Henry! Wake up out of your daydreaming and pay attention! The important part is coming," Homer said with the tenacity of a chihuahua. As Henry had drifted off ever so slightly, Alvin had slipped into a seat at the table. Henry got up, poured coffee into Alvin's cup, retrieved a bowl of freshly cut fruit and granola, and placed it in front of him.

"Okay, here's the deal, Homer. And you too, Henry." Alvin was about to explain his secret business plan that he worked on most of the night.

"Sword fights and dungeons. That's the key. An experiential medieval castle right here in Grace." Alvin beamed with a toothy smile.

"That's it? I was hoping for something a bit more sedate and dignified. Maybe some beautiful gardens with ponds hosting a couple of white swans. But, if you think that violence is the way to go, well, I am willing to listen, I guess." Homer had a hard time imagining how he would fare in Alvin's world. Sword runs through Homer, or, even more dramatically, he would be beheaded. Homer had no false illusions about what life would have been like for him in medieval Europe. He didn't think he would have been a king anyway. Or a prince. Most likely a poor, malnourished monk or the town fool. So, he was not yet warm to Alvin's fantasy idea.

"Well, I think it has some potential," Henry said. "I mean kids like video games, especially the virtual reality ones, better than TV and movies. It's all about the experience. Maybe if you make it feel real, then you will have a winner."

"Exactly, and we could run several subsidiary businesses off the main one. Suppose the main business is visiting the castle with a prisoner experience and a swordfight or two. In that case, you can run the concessions, winery, swords and shields merchandise, horse riding, rafting, minigolf, and keepsake pictures, all as secondary high-margin profit centers. Even my business. We could have a subsidiary office at the castle and provide boot camp and sword fighting training for the more athletic participants."

"Well, what constitutes the core business?"

"The castle is number one. It has to look and feel real. None of that fake Styrofoam stuff. Real stones, weathered, looking a thousand years old." Alvin had become surprisingly engaged in just one night. "Next is the moat. Around the castle with at least one drawbridge. Preferably two. And it needs to be linked to a water supply. You have a free-flowing creek on your land, so that should work. Next, you have to have some horses. You have llamas, alpacas, goats, and pigs. All good, but you need horses and maybe even some cows. Next, you need to clean up the nearby forest and make it walkable. You will need some wagons pulling visitors through the woods and some roving bandits who can shoot live arrows at them. Beyond those basics, well, we can use our imagination. Mongols, Vikings, Celts, Goths, Moors. We could hire a lot of people to attack the fortress. Maybe that would be the premium experience. And we would have to think seriously about catapults hurling fire and brimstone." Alvin was animated and on his feet by this point. Homer had never seen Alvin quite like this.

"What is brimstone exactly?" Henry asked innocently.

"Burning sulfur. The yellow sulfur catches fire and burns with an intense blue flame, turning into a brown gooey substance as it burns. And it gives off the foulest of odors that turns to acid on contact with moisture, like in a person's lungs."

Alvin was now transformed into a medieval sage strutting around with hands aloft in the coffee shop. The transformation was total and unexpected. Maybe Alvin had been Othello or Merlin in another life. After a few minutes, he calmed down, and Homer felt compelled to investigate a little further.

"Alvin, you seem to like this castle business more than I thought you would. Why?'

"My favorite game as a kid was Dungeons and Dragons. I got one of the first basic sets in 1977 for Christmas. My uncle in Atlanta got it for me. I loved it and played every day, even by myself. This castle business seems to reawaken some of those memories, I guess. I loved it then but stopped playing when I went into sports."

"You mean when you got your growth spurt! And why didn't you ever tell me about it? This is the first I ever heard that you liked that game."

"My mom thought it was devil worship. She threw it in the trash. But that night, I fished it out and hid it in a secret place so she wouldn't know. I played by myself, except when I went to visit my uncle in Atlanta. He and I would play all night."

"Never knew that about you, Alvin!" Henry finally joined the conversation. "What was your character name?" Henry asked.

"Modroc the Invincible. What about you?" Alvin could sense Henry might be a fellow player.

"Zeus the Thunder God," Henry said proudly.

The two middle-aged men discussed a game that they hadn't played in over thirty years for ten minutes. Homer was dumbfounded as he suddenly was not a party to what appeared to be an enjoyable conversation at the end of which the two men shared a secret handshake.

"Can we get back to the castle?" Homer bellowed.

"Well, we are going to need a lot of capital to pull this off. What investors do you have lined up, Homer?" Alvin looked at Homer with a quizzical stare.

"One. Realistically, how much do we need?"

Alvin reached into his leather briefcase and pulled out a ½ inch thick file. He flipped through several pages, sometimes smiling, sometimes frowning. He looked up at Homer and then at Henry.

"My estimate is we need $21,000,000 to get started. Then we need at least $4,000,000 annually in operating capital. So, the first year it's $25,000,000 total. Need about 200,000 visitors a year to break even on the yearly expenses."

Homer was captivated as Alvin explained the numbers and how he came up with the estimates. Homer's back-of-the-envelope calculations weren't a lot different. Homer knew that he didn't have that much money available, nor could he quickly borrow it without putting himself at exceedingly high risk. Now he wondered whether the tennis courts were still a good idea. Tennis seemed to be a distraction if the plan was to move forward with the castle. He would have to talk with Vladimir first. But, hopefully, nothing had been done on the tennis courts. Homer engaged back in the conversation for a few minutes and then excused himself to head back home, while Henry and Alvin got to know each other even better by comparing their Dungeons and Dragons experiences.

CHAPTER 16

▲

MANLY CONVERSATIONS

Jack Lincoln was short and a little chubby. His hair was mostly gone, and he wore wire-rimmed glasses with very thick lenses. At eighty-nine years of age, he had a limp from an old war injury, and he walked with a bit of a stooped-over gait. But, his mind was clear, his voice firm, and all his teeth were still his own. And he would provide Vladimir with expert advice.

"Jack. Over here."

Jack drove up in his beat-up twenty-year-old Chevy pickup. He stepped out and was walking toward the house when Vladimir called out. Despite his limp, Jack switched direction with the smoothness of a younger man. He took quick steps as if his life depended on getting to where he had to go. Vladimir and Mikhail met him by a pile of dirt and grass. Jack looked out over the ¼ acre of scraped earth. He shook hands with Mikhail and Vladimir as he surveyed the area without taking his eyes off the scraped ground.

"Vladimir, how many courts are you putting in here?" he asked, puzzled.

"Three."

"Okay. Need to widen out some to have more border on the outer courts."

"Yes. What else do you see?" Vladimir asked.

"You are going to need six poles and lights if you want to play at night. So, we should budget for that, and you're going to need to lay a power line in here to light things up." Jack turned around, scanning the house and the nearby buildings to see the power line. "You know, I think you need LED lights up here, and you should be able to use standard 120-volt lines." Vladimir followed everything that Jack was saying. And it was good to have someone with this knowledge to help. They walked around the area where the courts would be, and Jack pulled out his 75-foot measuring tape. He barked out numbers, and Mikhail wrote down everything. After about an hour, the three men sat down at the picnic table and made the necessary calculations. "Everything together, about $25,000. I think you can build it for that."

"Jack, that sounds exceptionally good. That's much less than I thought it would be, and Mr. Homer will be incredibly pleased—that's assuming you are going to do the work. That's just materials and the concrete truck."

"Yes, I understand."

Then the threesome walked out into the pasture and looked around the property. The tree line was about 100 feet back from the courts. Vladimir showed Jack where the property line ended up the hill in the woods. Then they walked over to the little stream. They discussed diverting some of the water into a pond and the requirements for a small dam. They walked the length of the creek on the property until they came upon the barn for the llamas and alpacas, where some of the animal feed and hay was stored. Thinking that it might be feeding time, the alpacas came running toward the barn but stopped when they saw Vladimir, who stepped out from behind Mikhail. Vladimir reached up to the lead alpaca, gave him a little tap on the nose, and they took off, running back out into the field. Vladimir would have to think about how to handle them once Mikhail was gone. Maybe Boris could take over.

Jack looked back at the house and noticed that the land between the alpaca barn and the house was very flat. Vladimir asked Jack questions about building a large home without revealing that it might be a castle. Jack was direct in his answer.

"Your best location, by far, is this pasture. You could build a vast structure, have good level ground to work with, and excellent sightlines and drainage. That's where I would put it," Jack said.

What Vladimir liked most was that Jack didn't ask unnecessary questions. Like why are you building a larger house? He simply answered the questions asked of him. They were both practical and prudent men who liked to build and work outside. After a couple of hours of working on the tennis court plans, concrete calculations, and layout of a pond and large house in what was currently the pasture, the men headed into the house for dinner. Homer recognized Jack and came over to give the official greeting. As they talked, it came out that Vladimir had innocently revealed the plan for a large home, if not a castle.

"So, you heard about my idea of a larger home—well, actually more like a castle. What do you think?" Homer asked.

"The best place to build the home, or castle, would be right out in that pasture." Jack was direct. No nonsense. He didn't pontificate on the merits of a castle. No, the only thing he could contribute at this point was the location.

"I see," Homer said. "What if I acquired more land around here, would there be a better site?"

"Depends on how much land you acquired. The hill on the other side of the pasture has a relatively flat top. A castle there would be seen from a long way off but would be harder to build. Hauling stuff up the hill would be a chore, and water supply issues could come up possibly."

"So, with the land, we have now, it's that pasture." Homer got up from the table and pointed out the bay window in the dining room.

"Yes, sir."

"How big a footprint can we have for the castle?" Homer asked.

"Now, that's a tough question that Vladimir and I pondered. Maybe up to a 100-foot square. About 10,000 square feet on the ground floor. Bigger than that, and you might have some problems with erosion from the creek. But of course, it would depend on the layout. Square versus rectangular or any other shape, for that matter."

As the three men plus Mikhail discussed building tennis courts and castles, they walked out onto the patio and sat down in wicker chairs by the pool. Valentina brought out some drinks and a salmon coulibiac she made while the men kept talking and laughing and enjoying the camaraderie. Valentina and the girls had the dining room to themselves and enjoyed talking about the day while they ate their slices of coulibiac. Boris had a couple of friends from school, and they wandered off to battle in their video games. All around, a wholesome night at the Pitts-Agapov estate.

Vladimir, curious, asked Jack about his limp.

"Got it in 1965 in the Vietnam War. I was in the Agency for International Aid, not the military. I was pretty much a pacifist back then and still am to some extent. People wrongly think that old white guys like me are all hawkish and want to go to war. Not me. Anyway, I was near the DMZ delivering rice to a village when the Viet Cong attacked the convoy. A grenade nearly took my leg off. I was knocked out. When I came to, I was the only one left alive. The Viet Cong had bayoneted all the wounded ones except me. Maybe they thought I was dead. I don't know. But I was found by some American GIs and medevaced out. I recuperated in a Philippine hospital and then returned to the States. I served out my term at the Aid Agency and figured I had paid my dues. I lived in San Francisco for a while before I met my wife. Got married sort of late. I was already thirty-six when my firstborn child came into the world. Never figured my wife would go before me." Jack stopped before he became tearful. He missed his wife terribly, and when he let himself think about her, he cried.

After a silence, Vladimir spoke first. "Thank you, Jack, for sharing this experience with us. I, too, was in a war." Vladimir couldn't say anymore either. The silence returned.

Homer stood up and lifted his drink for a serious toast.

"To those who have endured the agony of war, who have survived and prospered in life, and who remember the price paid by those who did not. Let us celebrate courage and life, and the love that keeps us human!" Homer drank a sip, and Vladimir led the cheer with a shout of "zazdarovye," the Russian phrase for "to your health," as they raised their glasses to toast and drink. Russians loved to toast and were good at it. Homer had enjoyed learning the art from the Agapovs.

Across town, another manly conversation was underway between Sheriff Meeks, Major Lowman, and the Reverend J.T. Jackson at the reverend's home. The major and the former sheriff came to the reverend's house to discuss a proposition. They wanted the minister to join them in a new endeavor.

"So, as I understand it, you want to expand the History Museum? Is that right?" the reverend opened.

"Not just expand, but redefine," the major responded as the director of the museum.

"Well, then I believe the three of us have a common goal here. We want to tell the story of Grace, Georgia, accurately and without embellishment. Is that right?" the reverend asked.

"Yes, but where to start? Was there ever a battle here in Grace?" Major Lowman asked the question that most interested a military man.

"Major Lowman, yes, there was. It happened over there on ole Homer's homestead," the reverend answered.

"Oh Lord, not there again. It seems like everything in Grace happens with, through, for, or against Homer Pitts!" Sheriff Meeks was beside himself.

"What kind of battle was it? Revolutionary War? Civil War?" Major Lowman ignored the Sheriff's protest.

"It was the Civil War. The Skirmish of Little Creek. At least that's what it was called back then. That creek on Homer's property is only six feet wide. And it's only about two feet deep at its deepest. But it moves pretty fast," Reverend Jackson said, having heard the story many times as a boy right before sleep as told by his ancient grandmother, Bessie. "Anyway, two Union deserters came to the creek to let their horses drink some water. They had been in the big battles already in Chickamauga and Kennesaw Mountain. Atlanta was burning, and Sherman turned east and was headed toward Savannah. These two Union boys had had their fill of killing and were riding back through the woods to go home to Ohio. There were two Confederate boys from Tennessee, and they were deserting too. They came riding up beside the creek on the other side. Neither the Union boys nor the Confederate boys had any powder for their guns, so when they met at the creek, they started hitting each other with the butts of their rifles. After a while, they realized that there wasn't any point in fighting. So, they sat down by the creek and just talked. All four of them got along so well that they called a truce and spent the night there. The next day the four of them rode up to Chattanooga. The two Confederate boys rode on up to Knoxville, where they were from, and the two Union boys rode on up to Cincinnati. You could say it was the first peace agreement of the war."

Major Lowman, intrigued, would have to research and verify the story's facts, but thought it might make a nice diorama for the museum. "Reverend, that's an interesting story. Do you know if there are any records to confirm it?"

"Major, it was told to me by my Grandmother Bessie, and I think that's all the verification it needs. She was well thought of and knowledgeable about history. People trusted her. God rest her soul!"

"Well, I am sure that she was, Reverend. I remember her," former Sheriff Meeks said. "Didn't she used to live out there near the drive-in theatre that showed those porno movies? The theatre that they turned into a graveyard. I bet you could see those things from her kitchen window. She could have charged admission, I suspect."

There was silence and a blush on the reverend's face. "She did live out near the cemetery. You're right." The reverend answered without besmirching his long-dead, dear grandmama or commenting on the price of admission Grandmama charged.

Lowman perceived that this wasn't the time or place to challenge the integrity of the story. And he wasn't sure whether the diorama should be in the town center where the history museum was now, or maybe it should be out at Homer's property, the site of the battlefield. These were details that would need to be addressed. But for now, all three men agreed that they should begin preparations for considering a Civil War battle exhibit somewhere.

The reverend's wife, Sally, made a funky stew and some brownies for their dinner. The stew was complete with chickpeas, carrots, potatoes, corn, and lima beans. Onions and garlic, pepper, and lots of fresh-baked bread to go with it. The stew was vegetarian but otherwise pretty standard. It was the mushrooms that made it funky. Sally picked them herself up in the North Georgia mountains with some old friends of hers.

Sally was a hippie chick in the early 1970s. She converted to disco later, but first, she was a hippie. Sally was "cool," with purple glasses and lots of beads, a ponytail, tie-dyed shirt, shorts, sandals, and a peace-sign necklace hanging around her neck. Long skinny legs and arms. She met the reverend when he was a long-haired, beard-wearing liberal theology student. Camouflage jacket, headband, sunglasses, bell bottoms, Birkenstocks, and dashiki shirt. They enjoyed the time, culture, and each

MANLY CONVERSATIONS

other. And then disco came, and a new wardrobe was acquired. And new music. But they remained fond of their hippie clothes.

The three guys started eating. After the first bowl of the delicious stew, they all sat back, took a deep breath, and then started talking again as they waited for their second bowls.

"Guys, I would take it easy on more stew. I mean, I will bring it if you want, but really, I would go slow," Sally said.

"We are hungry men, wife. Now bring us our stew!" the reverend proclaimed, a bit out of character.

Sally looked at him like the imbecile he was. "Yep. Okay."

"What about textiles? Weren't there some textile mills here? Could we create an exhibit on textiles here in Grace?" Lowman asked.

"Well, that's a good idea," the sheriff volunteered. "The old textile plant is where the antique mall is now. So, that's another place we could put a museum. Out at the antique mall."

"What about famous people? Can we have some exhibits with them?" Lowman was on a roll.

"Well, I think the two most famous people from Grace are Alvin Teabody and Homer Pitts. So we could talk with them and maybe put them in an exhibit," the reverend said.

"Let's recap. A central museum in the town square. A satellite battlefield out at Homer's. And a textile annex at the antique mall. Is that right?" Lowman felt he was on to something big.

"Yes, sounds like it. Do you think it's a little excessive?" the reverend questioned while having an unusual twitch of his left eyelid. The major and the sheriff stared at the reverend as the twitch spread to his right eyelid.

"Yes, I think it sounds excessive," Meeks said cautiously as the reverend's lips began to quiver too.

"Well, what should I do about it?" Lowman asked.

"Let's just focus on expanding here in the town center. We have an extra room with some good lighting. What we need are some artifacts. Do we have any?" Meeks asked as the twitching died down without the reverend ever acknowledging his unusual facial movements.

"Well, we have this can that was found out at Homer's place. In the creek. It looks a little like a beer can, but I wonder if it could be a ration can from the Civil War skirmish? What do you think?" Lowman held up the can and agreed that it did resemble a beer can. "The county jail cleanup crew pulled the can out of the creek as they cleaned it at Homer's request six months earlier. They also found an old bullet that some hunters thought came from a modern hunting rifle, maybe a 30-06 bolt-action rifle. Homer gave them to the Historical Society for safekeeping." The reverend thought both items looked like Civil War vintage. And so, it went back and forth between the three men. After finishing their second bowls of stew, they talked a little more and then asked Sally if she could give them a little more stew. Third bowls, half full, all around. The stew was delicious, and all three felt good. Really good.

"Guys, take it easy on the stew," Sally warned again. She thought that the reverend and his buddies should understand that wild North Georgia mushrooms were best enjoyed in small quantities.

"Wench, get me my stew!" the reverend commanded. The other two guys looked at the reverend with some trepidation. Sally just shrugged her shoulders and mouthed, "Okay."

MANLY CONVERSATIONS

"Sheriff, have you ever noticed that you have a very long face?" the reverend asked innocently. As he asked, he noticed that not only did the sheriff have a long face, but it started moving like a wave.

"Now Reverend, you know I am not the sheriff anymore, and my face has probably disappeared. It's floating over there in the corner. Oops, it just flew out the window!" the former sheriff said. All three men looked at each other and started laughing hysterically. They laughed so hard that they each fell backward in their chairs. As they scrambled to stand up, each one had a slightly different problem. The major screamed out that gravity had attacked him and was holding him down. And that since gravity was invisible, he couldn't see how to get gravity off.

"Here, Major, I will hit gravity," proclaimed the reverend, who promptly took a broom and swatted gravity right on the back as it hovered over the major's face. But the broom flew through gravity and hit the Major right on the head.

"Oops!" both the reverend and the sheriff started laughing hysterically again, but the major was out cold. The two conscious men began to chase each other around the house, playing pin the tail on the donkey. Sally was out back by the pool with a tray of brownies, relaxing. Their teenage kids wouldn't be home until later, so this was her quiet time. Sally wondered if maybe the stew was loaded with too many of the wild mushrooms she picked.

The guys were having so much fun that they forgot about the brownies until around 11 p.m. Sally rationed them out one brownie each, including the major who had now awakened after his little interlude with gravity and unconsciousness. She monitored the men as they enjoyed the dessert, and a little while later, all three were pretty relaxed. Around midnight, she made the executive decision to confiscate all three sets of car keys from the men, and then she went off to bed. The ex-sheriff went to sleep in a Lay-Z-Boy chair in the reverend's den. He went sound asleep, enjoying his weird, flashing, psychotropic dreams. He fidgeted and called out a few times during the night but mostly slept. The major wandered into the garage and passed out over the Reverend's washing machine, where he relieved himself of the night's dinner directly into the washing machine tub. And then he stayed put, hugging the washing machine and snoring all night. The reverend tried to follow his beautiful wife upstairs but fell face-first down on the stairwell. He didn't get hurt or knocked out, but he did go to sleep almost immediately. It was the best sleep he had had in years.

The next morning.

"Oh, no, my God! Daddy is dead! Daddy is dead! Call 911! Call 911!" Sally screamed, standing at the top of the stairs as she beheld a non-moving Leland on the stairs. Once she heard his snores, her mood changed. She was now disgusted and slapped him on the head.

"Get up, Leland. What's wrong with you? Get up! Get up!" She ran into the kitchen, got a pitcher of ice and water, and ran back to the stairs. She checked to make sure he was breathing. Once she confirmed that he was still alive, she poured the entire pitcher onto the reverend's head. He bolted up and ran around the house with water and ice cubes going everywhere. Once she calmed down, Sally dissolved into tearful appeals for forgiveness for poisoning her husband and his friends while the reverend fell back asleep on the couch in the den. Both Major Lowman and Sheriff Meeks slept a little later and then had abrupt awakenings, but neither had a pitcher of ice water on their heads, either. They gathered their things and headed out to their cars after retrieving their keys from Sally.

Sally headed over to the couch. "Leland, Leland, wake up. Please, baby, wake up. Oh, forgive me. I should have never given you that second bowl, much less the third or the brownies. This is all my fault!"

The reverend snored and turned on his side. And continued to sleep.

After Sally got through screaming that the reverend had died and then asking for forgiveness, she settled back into a more copasetic demeanor with her coffee at the kitchen table. Alone. The reverend finally woke up with a sour look on his face and then suddenly bounded up the stairs to the Master bathroom, loudly heaving and purging the demons of the previous night. After embracing the toilet for several minutes, he took a hot shower and felt he just might make it.

When he was back downstairs, Sally had a question.

"Leland, do you remember the Theta House?" Sally asked as Leland walked into the kitchen.

"Wow, what a night," the reverend said. He meant the previous night, not the fifty-year-old faded memory of his college days.

"Leland, what did you drink that night at the Theta House? Do you remember?" Sally had an irritating habit of dredging up some long-ago humiliation to frame her dismay with a recent misstep. Irritating but highly effective.

"Sally, you know that I had four tequila sunrises that night and that I was sick for two days. And I embarrassed myself in front of the whole crowd. I get your point. Forgive me for my rudeness last night."

"Rudeness. Yeah. But you also embarrassed yourself in front of your daughter. She had a good laugh this morning. So, what happened?" Sally inquired.

"It was nice to talk with the guys. The stew was good, but we were just having a good time." Leland enjoyed himself, feeling young again.

"Okay. Well, I am glad you had the guys over, and you had a good conversation. I don't appreciate being called a wench, though."

The reverend blushed at the mention of "wench." His recollection was vague and distorted.

"Sorry," he said.

They stared at each other for a moment. Then they burst into laughter. Sally had said her peace and was relaxed now.

The reverend finished an orange juice and a piece of dry toast. He was gradually getting back to normal. He headed to his study where he checked his list of tasks for the day. But his thoughts kept going back to the discussion from the night before. The guys would need to go out to Homer's and explore the creek for artifacts. That would be fun, and Major Lowman had a brilliant idea to invite two other guys to join their little group—Dr. Hippo and Dr. Youssef. The two doctors didn't know the other three men very well, but all five would have an opportunity to bond as they set about prospecting for Civil War relics.

Major Lowman sat quietly in his office on the town square. He put up a detailed topographic map of the town, including Homer's land. The creek was on the map, and the hill was nearby. He went back to the copy of the letter he found in an online archive based in Tennessee. The letter was from one of the Northern soldiers to the Southern soldier twenty years after their little fight. He was recounting the day and night they spent at that little creek. He mentioned walking up the hill to get some firewood. He saw a little cave between two large granite boulders and thought they should hide in there for a while. But the following day, they all decided to head north to Chattanooga. The letter concluded with a wish for peace and remembrance as the two men got older. Major Lowman read the letter several times to glean any clues he could about the activities and thoughts of the four men. He felt connected to them each time he read it, and he thought it would be a great centerpiece to the exhibit.

Sheriff Meeks was connected as well. He enjoyed meeting with the other guys and doing some stuff together. He wasn't much of a historian, but he could dig pretty well. His summer job as a teenager was digging ditches. Other than that job, he had been a law enforcement officer his entire adult life. Now he would be something different. But another thought was on his mind these days. Connie Marlboro. She was a pretty little firecracker, and he hoped they would see each other before too long, especially now that his ribs were healing.

CHAPTER 17

▲

NOVEMBER 1963

On a cold November 1963 weekend, the train ride back to Georgia from New York City took two days. Being back among the pines and farmland was depressing. She missed New York City. And the love of her life. She didn't know that it would work out that way. She didn't know that she wouldn't see him again. When you are young, you take for granted that you will get another chance to love and see sights and travel. To be what you always wanted to be. To chase your passion. You think that the next opportunity will be just around the corner, that it won't be long. She felt all those emotions. She also felt a terrible pain in leaving him with no contact information and no way to stay in touch. She looked in her purse. Yes, his card was still there. She picked it up from the side table at the hotel before she left him that morning while it was still dark. The card had his company's name and address. She would write to him when she got back home. Maybe in a month or two. Right now, she had to prepare herself for the return. She had to go back to Grace to settle things. Do it right before she could ever move on to something else.

Return to her forty-year-old husband, "the Old Man," and his three teenage sons. She was a young bride to a much older man, previously married. Betrothed by her Mama after her Pa died, and her Mama was dying. Mama didn't listen, and she wanted her girl to "stay out of trouble." Old-world style. Angelina hated the process if not the man to whom she was given. She wanted to travel and to be something. But instead, she was sent to do what poor wives do. The laundry and the cooking and the cleaning. So that's what she did when she was seventeen while her Ma was still alive.

At nineteen, after her Ma had passed, Angelina left for New York City. She left the Old Man a note on that sticky, hot July morning. In a place where he would find it when he awoke from his drunken stupor after a night of carousing. And she made sure she was on the train going north before he would wake up and find the note. She made the train and then sat for two days on a hard seat, feeling freedom ooze into her soul with every mile of pine trees and farmhouses that passed by. She arrived in the most fantastic city on earth and somehow navigated herself, as many migrants before had, to a shared apartment and a waitressing job. She left Georgia with nothing except a couple of dresses and a will to work. In the big, bustling city, she found a stable place to stay and had a little money in her pocket after a few weeks. And the last three months that she spent there were the happiest of her life because she found love. A love that became a cherished memory that she would never forget. But Angelina also knew that she had to return to Grace at least until she could get a divorce from the Old Man and, maybe, get her land back. The land that her mama had given the Old Man. Fate—such a fickle thing. To escape a created hell only to return voluntarily a few months later. Her emotions were storming, and she wrestled with it all so much that it made her sick.

NOVEMBER 1963

The nausea she was having was new. Maybe motion sickness on top of everything else. She went to the toilet on the train a couple of times, but she could only gag. It passed after a while. Just an hour more on the train, and she would be back at the train station from where she had started five months earlier. She would have to catch a ride out to the house or walk. It was all so primitive compared to New York, but it didn't matter. This was her fate and where she needed to be. The Old Man and the stepsons might hate her for leaving, but they wouldn't refuse her cooking, cleaning, or washing clothes. She sat by the window on the train and looked at the passing pine trees and farmland again. The sun was rising after a long rattling night of train riding. And she thought for the next hour about what she was giving up.

CHAPTER 18

GOOD NEWS AND BAD NEWS

"Count, we have the test results. Some good news, some bad news." Archie said matter-of-factly.

"Bad news first," The Count answered.

"The results are inconclusive."

"Disappointing. The good news?"

"You and Mr. Pitts are a 98.9% match," Archie said in a more optimistic tone.

"What? I thought you said that they were inconclusive."

"They are. In a court of law, anything less than 99% is considered inconclusive to establish paternity. Anything above 0% means you have not been excluded either," Archie explained.

"Well, what would boost this up above 99%?" the Count asked.

"We could try another sample, but there is only one thing that would make a meaningful impact."

"What is it?"

"The mother's DNA," Archie said solemnly. "And the other terrible news, I am afraid, is that Angelina died three years ago. Cancer. I am sorry Count to have to tell you."

In a moment of silence on the phone, the Count contemplated the implications of Archie's words. The Count never really imagined her passing. She was younger than he, and in his mind, she was still that young, vivacious beauty he had met so long ago. The sudden news unleashed demons the Count had carried for decades. He didn't wake up in time to stop her. He didn't chase after her to the only train heading to Georgia. He let her go. He should have known that's where she would go. He should have pursued her. But he was full of himself back then. He thought that, of course, she would come back to him. Or that he would just move on.

The office moved from New York to London, and he went with it. Outside on his balcony at the Lake Geneva home with beauty and splendor in front of him, tears rolled down his cheeks. He stood with the phone as Archie waited in silence. Standing on the balcony in the afternoon sun, warm and inviting, he felt so alone. So terribly cheated of the years of bliss he never had. He could still see her young, tanned face and her blue eyes sparkling. Her lips that he would gently touch with his. Her smell, her warmth. It all was just too much for him to bear at this moment.

"Okay. Let me think about this a bit, and I will call you back. I need to go now. Au revoir." He hung up quickly and finally sat down, alone, looking out over the magnificent lake, with the sun warming his old, fragile body and his tortured soul. And he wept.

The Count, later called Archie, once had grieved his loss. And he gave Archie the go-ahead.

"Mr. Pitts, this is Archie DeSaliere from London. I am calling again to follow up with you regarding our recent visit together."

GOOD NEWS AND BAD NEWS

"Yes, Mr. DeSaliere, so good to talk with you."

"I am calling to convey greetings from Count Armand St. Clare. The Count lives in Geneva and is my employer. He would like to invite you to visit with him at his home on Lake Geneva. We would like you to come next week, and if you can come, we will take care of all arrangements for travel and lodging at no cost to you. I know this is short notice, but I believe this opportunity is a perfect one for both you and the Count."

"Thank you, Mr. DeSaliere, but I don't know the Count, but I did read a recent article about him in a New York magazine. Nice piece. But, you know I don't usually travel on short notice to Europe just because someone would like to meet me? Could we have a phone call or maybe a video chat first?" Homer was polite but noncommittal.

"Mr. Pitts, I understand your reservation. Let me put it this way. The Count is the sole owner of a large multinational company, Suisse St. Clare. He is a billionaire many times over and is near ninety years of age. Having people come to him in Switzerland is particularly important to him. Should I let him know that you will be able to come?"

Homer was stunned. Why would a Swiss billionaire whom he didn't know invite him to Switzerland? What could this possibly be about? Homer didn't know, but it sounded exciting and more than a little mysterious. So, of course, he said yes, after carefully negotiating some of the particulars.

"So, that's a yes, Mr. Pitts," a nearly exasperated Archie said after their thirty-minute negotiation. " You will leave Tuesday and return Sunday, midday flights, first-class, chauffeured limo to and from, and some special orders for in-flight meals and drinks. Does that sound correct?"

"Why indeed, yes, Mr. Desaliere. I look forward to meeting the Count."

"Excellent."

"And one last question, should I bring people with me, or is this just me coming?"

"Just you, Mr. Pitts."

"And one final question. What is the reason for this trip?" Homer asked delicately.

"To be discussed in Switzerland. But suffice it to say, it's about the past and the future, and a great opportunity," Archie responded.

"Okay. Sounds mysterious, but I am looking forward to it."

The phone disconnected, and Homer mused as to the reason for the visit. Maybe it was something to do with his fashion days. He didn't speculate too much. He had so much to do at the estate. He needed to walk up the little mountain on the other side of the field to find that opening to the cave of his youth, that little hideout where he and Gabriel Montcliff hid during games they played when Homer was visiting the wealthiest people in Grace. Homer wanted to find the cave again after decades because he had had dreams about Gabriel for the last few weeks. They were becoming more frequent and more vivid. Maybe it was reminiscing about Mama that brought them on. Or perhaps something else. But they were unsettling him. He hadn't had the dreams for several decades, and why they would suddenly return mystified him. And he had made a point over the last few years to never go near that cave for fear of reigniting the dreams. So now that they were back, it was imperative to return to the cave of his youth. Where Gabriel, his best friend, died.

CHAPTER 19

▲

THE MONTCLIFFS

The Montcliffs ran the town of Grace for several decades. They owned the textile mill where most townspeople worked and the company store where millworkers could buy groceries and hardware and put it on their charge accounts until the next paycheck. The Montcliffs built a church in town and the little town hall. The Montcliffs also built the school where their children and the rest of the town's kids went. Homer, Alvin, and Gabriel, the youngest Montcliff, became friends at school. Gabriel invited Homer and Alvin to come out to play most weekends until they were eleven. Gabriel, Alvin, and Homer played in the creek and the woods and hid in the cave on the Montcliff property.

The cave was halfway up the little mountain beyond the large meadow at the Montcliffs. An opening between two large granite boulders led to an inner cavern carved by water oozing in and cutting through the underlying limestone. The cave extended deeply into the mountain and narrowed down to a narrow opening that only small people could squeeze—no normal-sized adults. Homer and Gabriel would squeeze through very carefully, and they could see that the little stream spilled out like a waterfall, deep into the darkness. Cave spiders and bats pestered them, but Gabriel insisted that they had to continue exploring. By age eleven, Alvin was growing faster than either Homer or Gabriel, and he couldn't fit into the cave anymore. But Homer and Gabriel, still small, kept going into the cave's little waterfall opening until they were twelve.

At twelve, the Montcliffs sent their kids off to private boarding schools. An elite education for elite young kids. Gabriel was the last in a long line of Montcliff children. Six before him, three boys and three girls. All went off to the elite schools. His mother and father traveled extensively, and he was usually in the care of Miss Ferguson, the live-in nanny. He didn't see his siblings much, and Homer's feelings of being an only child were not foreign to Gabriel. Gabriel and Homer planned to use a rope to lower themselves down the waterfall deeper into the cave one weekend. They didn't tell anyone, even Alvin, to fear that the adults would think it was too risky and stop them from true spelunking. That weekend, Homer had to stay home, in isolation, because he had chickenpox. So, Homer couldn't go with Gabriel into the cave to spelunk, leaving Gabriel to spelunk alone. By the time he was better and out of isolation, Gabriel had been missing for ten days. The police looked everywhere, and the family was distraught. After a month, the family gave up with no sign of Gabriel and no ransom note from a kidnapper. They let their little boy go—his empty casket buried in the Grace Memorial Gardens. The mansion faded, Miss Ferguson retired, and the Montcliffs moved to Naples, Florida.

Homer told the Montcliffs that Gabriel would be in the cave. They looked, but Homer knew they didn't look hard enough or believe he could crawl into the tiny opening in the rocks where the waterfall was. Adults were like that. The adults felt sorry for Homer's and Alvin's grief and didn't believe their stories about the cave and how Gabriel believed there was treasure there and that the cave extended for miles under the mountains. The adults thought that the stories were just the little fictions children created when they hurt. They patted Homer's head and told him he would get over it in time. Homer never forgot Gabriel. He lost track of the Montcliffs, and they put Grace out of their memories. But Homer knew that one day he would look for Gabriel again in the cave.

CHAPTER 20

▲

CONSTRUCTION AND CELEBRATION

Vladimir, Mikhail, and Jack worked hard for the next few days. They cleared the ground and dug the five-inch foundation for the tennis courts. A cement truck poured enough concrete to create one massive slab for the three courts and the surrounding area with some expansion joints placed to prevent cracking. They spread the acrylic coat over the entire slab to create the green playing surface. After it dried, the men painted the lines, erected fences, set poles, installed nets, and attached lights.

And then, after a week's work, on a Tuesday night, with a clear sky and warm summer air, Homer gave the privilege to flip the switch to Jack, Vladimir, and Mikhail. The whole family looked on along with Alvin, his wife Contessa, and their two boys, two girls, and Carl and Lula Bell, as they all prepared to shine the lights on the newest tennis courts in Grace. Of course, Homer hammed it up, teasing the crowd with antics, but the moment finally came. The three men flipped the big yellow switch together, and six giant LED lights burst forth with radiance over the new green courts. Alvin walked out on the court along with Carl. When Carl wasn't golfing, he played tennis. Alvin served, and Carl returned. It was a friendly demonstration—not a killer competition.

Everyone clapped. Then the Agapov girls and the Teabody kids took over the courts, whacking away. Mikhail, Boris, and Ludmilla weren't interested in tennis or sports, so they didn't join. Mikhail was focused on being a butler and would soon leave town to do that. Boris was a younger, smaller version of Mikhail, and he wanted to do the things his older brother did. Ludmilla wanted to be a scientist and doctor—an infectious disease doctor who studied killer bugs. For her, walking through the woods with Mikhail and Boris or by herself was what she liked—getting specimens to look at under the microscope. Or dissect. It was her passion. So, the brothers and sister sat out the tennis playing. Not with malice. They were happy for their sisters. But they were interested in other things.

Lula Bell had a friendly conversation with Contessa while all the other folks reveled in the new courts. Contessa was a tall woman with ebony skin, exquisite long hair, and a great mind. A native of Pittsburgh, Contessa met Alvin when he played football in New York, and she was a graduate student at Columbia. Love at first sight, and she never looked back. He was handsome and athletic, for sure. But she liked his no-nonsense, no-excuses, can-do spirit. His noble character was what caught her heart. They had been together ever since and suffered through some challenging moments like any couple. But, they found with each conflict something deeper to love and cherish in each other.

Now, Contessa was a professor of archeology at the University of Georgia. She commuted from Grace to Athens twice a week and spent most of her other time digging nearby Cartersville at the Etowah

CONSTRUCTION AND CELEBRATION

▲

Mounds site. She studied ancient Native American sites to discern their lifestyles and migration patterns. Occasionally, she would add short studies of Mesoamerican civilizations. But her primary work was in Georgia and the southeast. While Alvin was in Europe, she had filled a visiting professorship at Cambridge. She joined digs in Egypt and the Middle East with other professors before the Iraq and Afghanistan wars. Her further studies included native villages in Alaska and expeditions in Australia, exploring the aboriginal culture. Her two books were academic bestsellers, and undergraduate majors used her textbook throughout the US and Europe. This world-renown researcher and teacher would soon add a unique credential to her resume. She would become a founding member of the Grace Historical Excavation team from the Grace History Museum, transforming the gang of five into six. But that was to come. On this night at Homer's, she was just Alvin's wife on a summer evening at a friend's house, enjoying a celebratory picnic and enjoying her conversation with Lula Bell about the merits and shortcomings of men.

Homer was strangely quiet that evening, contemplating his travel to Switzerland. He hadn't shared the details with anyone. He wasn't sure why. Usually, it was the kind of thing that he would talk about and debate and ask folks what they thought. But he kept the conversations that he had with Archie to himself. No one knew on that evening that he would leave the following Tuesday for several days. The question he couldn't stop pondering was why a reclusive Swiss billionaire wanted to talk to him about some vague opportunity. And wanted to talk bad enough to fly Homer to Switzerland, all expenses paid.

Homer read online about the Count. The man was born in

Switzerland, educated in England at Cambridge and Oxford, and then in the US at Harvard. He lived in New York City and then in London, Tokyo, and Rio de Janeiro. And Istanbul. All to learn his father's diverse business operations in preparation to take over when his father died or retired. And then, when the Count did take over, he grew the privately-held company to enormous proportions. The Count had no descendants to carry on the St. Clare legacy into his eighties, except a rather dubious third cousin, twice removed, named Leopold.

What could this man possibly want with Homer? Maybe he read some of Homer's articles and books, and something in those musings interested him. Perhaps something in the video that went viral caught his eye. Style? Fashion? It didn't seem likely. Maybe something else. Homer enjoyed the idea that he would travel to a place to which he had never been. Perhaps he could arrange a little side trip to Zurich and Bern while visiting with the mystery man. Maybe a trip to Basel, with its annual world-renown art show. Even if not, it was still an international trip and would give him some new stories to tell and mysteries to tease. Then Homer thought about his finances.

The tennis courts cost less than he expected, thanks to Jack's wise counsel and the manual labor from Vladimir and Mikhail. But he would still need to trim expenses where he could. He could afford the tennis lessons for the girls and the butler school for Mikhail. And the new little laboratory hut for Ludmilla at the edge of the woods, where Homer was sure a Nobel Prize winner would be born. But the castle might be too much. He might have to, for once, trim back his idealism and grandiosity. Settle for something practical or nothing at all. And

CONSTRUCTION AND CELEBRATION

▲

that made him sad. He was a small man who liked to live a big life.

The celebration lasted until midnight, and then the tennis court lights were extinguished. The lights were off, which meant the loud hum they emitted was off too. Homer needed the quiet to sleep. This was the time of the year when he liked to have the windows throughout the house open. He had screens on the windows, and the fresh air moving through the halls and rooms was what cleansed the home of its winter staleness. This period only lasted a few weeks until the full summer heat set in later in June. High temperatures in the nineties, but more importantly, the high humidity of the South. Even here in Grace, closer to the Appalachians than the Gulf or the Atlantic. Even here, the moisture stifled life.

Southern air could wring out every bit of ambition and initiative a person had, especially at night when the air was soupy and unmoving. Homer grew up without an air conditioner. Fans could push the air around, but it was still hot, sticky, wet air that clung to you like superglue. The heat built up until your forehead was loaded with tiny drops of sweat, and your T-shirt and underwear were wet and dripping. And he remembered in his youth, lying in bed, with no cover or sheets or blankets, just lying there on top of the mattress that could feel like you were sinking into a lava bed in hell. Yes, during that part of the summer, you needed to close all the windows and let the air conditioner blow. When he bought the mansion, he installed two massive AC units to suck out every drop of water in the air and get the temperature down to arctic levels. It had been his dream to live in a home that required you to wear a sweater or sweatshirt amid the oppressive summer heat. Now that was progress, and Homer spared no expense to ensure that his summer was cool. But the best time of the year was still this interlude when the cooling breeze from outdoors was natural and pleasant, between the temperate winter and the summer Hades.

With open windows at night, there were also natural outdoor sounds. Spring peepers were pleasant, steady, and soothing. Grasshoppers and cicadas annoyed Homer with rising and falling volumes. An occasional owl hoot was pleasant. Barking dogs, not so. A passing jet from Hartsfield looping high overhead in a holding pattern as the world's busiest airport backed up—a marker for civilization, thus acceptable. A hot rod who just happened to pick Homer's country road to drive at eighty miles an hour gunning the doctored muffler beyond reason. They were not allowed.

Same for motorcycles. Homer alerted the state patrol's local officer that the patrol might reap some speeding violations by sitting on the road in front of Homer's house. Homer had Valentina walk across the pasture to carry the friendly patrolman some sandwiches and tea to seal the deal. With windows open at night, this time of year required the speeding teenage joyriders to be silenced for a few weeks. After the windows were closed again and the air conditioners returned, the speedsters could race all they wanted as far as Homer concerned, and the patrolman could protect other parts of the county. But during the spring, open windows interlude, no speedsters. And then there was the occasional bear growl.

Homer wasn't sure that the bear was on his land. Occasionally, when he couldn't sleep, and the windows were open, he would hear the growl. It would usually happen when Homer was nodding off,

CONSTRUCTION AND CELEBRATION

in the world between deep sleep and wakefulness. That world where strange sounds and impressions lived, and you weren't sure if the growl happened outside in the woods from a real bear or was manufactured by your brain cells.

On that night of the tennis extravaganza in the wee hours of the darkest part of the night, Homer was fully awake and heard it. It came fast, so Homer could only capture the last part of the growl in his consciousness. He was too slow to record it on his iPhone, and no matter how long he waited, it never came back. But Homer was sure he heard it. The following day, Mikhail would go out into the woods looking for evidence. He found a single smudged footprint down by the creek that could be a bear but was more likely from a big dog. Mikhail wasn't sure, but it was enough evidence for Homer. Bears were mystical, solitary creatures—a little like Homer. Maybe Homer had been a bear in another life. And then he finally drifted off to sleep.

CHAPTER 21

AWAY IN SWITZERLAND

Homer slept briefly on the overnight flight from Atlanta to Paris. His transit through Charles De Gaulle Airport to board the flight to Switzerland was quick and efficient. The flight was short, and as the jet slowed and began to drop toward Geneva, Homer could see mountain peaks through the clouds. Little squares of well-manicured farmland came into view, and a fuller picture of towering mountains just a litte off in the distance. A lake that initially appeared small became much more prominent as the jet descended. And as the plane prepared for landing, Homer could see the city on the lake's shore. The touchdown was soft and skipped until the plane made solid, final contact with the ground, letting him know he was in a differnt country. The unloading was efficient, and his trip through Customs proceeded without delay.

As he walked alone through the terminal, he marveled at the preciseness of everything—each little shop and display. Nothing out of order. He could read English, French, German, Italian, and even a little Romani amongst the various signs and posters around the terminal.

He had checked only one suitcase to pick up, and a man waited by the door with a placard that read "HOMER PITTS." Homer grabbed his bag and then approached the man. The man shook Homer's hand with a bear-like grip. A Russian probably—big and burly, curt but polite. Homer followed the man's lead out to a large Mercedes sedan and took a short drive through the city and then a long drive out into the countryside. It was as Homer imagined and as the pictures had shown. Manicured, tidy, pleasant, with towering, looming mountains further in the distance. Little farms and cottages spread about the countryside. After a twenty-minute drive, Homer could see a large estate in the distance. Maybe a hundred acres, he thought. A two-story main house with a red-tiled roof surrounded by patios and vineyards, with plaster walls and fountains. An estate that Homer saw in pictures in Architectural Digest as he researched the Count. It was a genuine European estate, maybe a few hundred years old, where the wealth was evident in everything that existed but never mentioned. To mention money in a place like that meant you weren't wealthy enough.

The Mercedes slowed and turned onto a gravel drive surrounded by oak trees, ancient and gnarled. A short hundred-foot drive and then an opening onto the motor courtyard. Like a birth of sorts, he was entering this new, elite world. The car came to a stop, and a real butler, refined and mustached, with graying slicked-back hair, opened Homer's door and invited him out into this new world. Homer exited the car, which the driver promptly parked in the nearby, detached garage on the other side of the motor courtyard. The driver took the suitcase out and then disappeared inside the mansion. The butler escorted Homer through the entrance with its centuries-old, weathered oak door. They walked down the marble-floored entry hall, entering the living room where Homer could see vineyards and fruit trees through the tall glass windows. The butler took Homer's carry-on bag and offered him a moist, warm towel as well as sparkling water. Homer took a seat in a comfortable-looking leather chair on the stone patio outside. Acres of a vineyard came into view, with glistening green and purple grapes. The smell of lavender and rosemary wafted toward Homer on a light breeze. A few moments of solitude and peace revived Homer's senses.

A well-preserved older man with only a little white hair, stylishly cut, came out onto the stone patio. His smooth, sun-kissed skin evidenced care and feeding with exquisite lotions. He wore a light tan sweater over a baby blue polo shirt. Plain dark trousers, comfortable loafers. Expensive but straightforward, including the blue and gold silk scarf around the Count's neck.

"Bonjour. I am Count Armand St. Clare," the old man said softly. He remained standing by Homer's chair with an outstretched hand. Homer stood up and gently accepted his hand. They were the same height.

"Homer Pitts," Homer responded. He felt nervous and edgy. This man was important to him, but he wasn't exactly sure why.

"Mr. Pitts, *merci beaucoup* for coming to my home. I know it was a long trip and that you are an important and busy man." The Count spoke softly and deliberately with an accent that was warm and accepting. Genuine kindness and peace were what Homer felt from this older man.

"Let us sit now." The older man fluidly sat in a leather chair opposite Homer. Homer sat as well.

"I have longed for this moment for a very long time, Homer. If I may call you that?"

"You may," Homer was cautious.

"Homer, you and I are connected by our love for an extraordinary woman. Your mother, Angelina, was the love of my life. A love that I let get away." Tears began to roll down his old face. Homer was shaken. He could not comprehend the meaning of what the Count was saying just yet.

"We shared a few months in New York. We shared a bed too. They were the most special days and nights of my life. And then she was gone from me." He paused and looked out toward the vineyard. The silent moment lingered. Homer looked at the man and could see the features. The short stature. The nose and brow. His hair was mostly gone, but its fineness was familiar. Homer knew before the Count murmured the words.

"Homer, I am your father. You are descended from your beautiful mother and me. I regret not knowing you—not raising you, but I am happy to be here now with you. I hope, with time, that you will be happy also."

"I am happy, Papa," the words spilled out from Homer naturally. He felt a rising joy, without having considered its deep meaning to Homer's life yet. "Joyous. I think that I have felt your presence my whole life. And now, I feel complete."

The older man, too, was filled with a joy that he could not have imagined. He lurched forward to hug Homer and Homer met him. The two men embraced, and the embrace lingered. Each man knew that when they backed away from each other, life would be different. The moment passed, and the men sat back down in their respective chairs.

"I must tell you, Homer, that when I first saw you on the video, I knew you were my son. I could see in your mannerisms and appearance a younger me."

"Well, Papa, we owe it all to an intoxicated sheriff, a llama named Horatio, and the swimming pool." They both chuckled at the video that had brought them together. They talked for a while about small things. How do you fill in a sixty year gap? Not all at once. They instinctively understood. The Count motioned for his butler, and the two men had lunch on the patio as the Count started to describe his life, love, and farm. After an afternoon together and then a light dinner, they walked out into the vineyard as twilight approached. The full moon shone brightly on the horizon, so they were in no hurry to go back inside. The Count related his years with the vineyard—the good years and the mediocre ones.

Homer asked questions and connected dots. They talked of Homer's mother. Of the letters, she sent the Count. And when they stopped. Homer described her final days and the funeral, all while they walked the vineyard. At the end of the vineyard, the ground rose to form a little hill where a stone bench stood guard. They sat down on the bench and looked over the estate. It wasn't large, not even as large as Homer's back in Grace. But its location was prime and worth tens of millions of dollars. The Count loved the family estate but made it clear to Homer that the house he had built on Lake Geneva was his first love. The Count informed Homer that they would travel to the lake house the following day. The Count also began to explain the specifics of his anguish about his legacy.

"I never found a love to replace my love for your mother. I never had my own family. And the St. Clare's are a long line of only children. Despite all my wealth, I don't have someone worthy to carry on the St. Clare legacy. Only a dim-witted third cousin twice removed named Leopold. He needs to be taken care of, not inheriting large estates and a multinational private company. But, until now, I have had no immediate living biological relative to follow me," the Count related to Homer. "Whatever joy living to old age and being very wealthy may have brought, it also meant for me that all of my family was already gone by the time I reached this moment in life—until you. I don't know if any of what has been done can be undone. I will see. But there is something I do want you to see tomorrow in Geneva. Something that I can share with you." The Count's privately held company exceeded several billion U.S. dollars in value. At present, the Count's will stipulated that Leopold would get the company and the Count's private real estate and assets if the Count died. This choice was increasingly unthinkable for the Count, but he needed a suitable alternative that Leopold or his handlers wouldn't challenge.

Homer and the Count walked back to the patio and sat by a fire where they were joined by the now casually dressed butler, the house chef, and a security guard, along with some wine and a few kinds of cheese, olives, cured ham, salami, and Swiss roggenbrot. Some shared jokes and stories brought laughter around the fire and lightened the mood. Around midnight, the little gathering broke up, and Homer was escorted to his bedroom. He showered and barely made it to the bed before he fell into a deep sleep.

Back at home, Vladimir was in charge while Homer was away.

Except in the kitchen where Valentina was in charge. And Mikhail was assigned to run the house. In a pinch, Carl could step in with advice. Alvin was a go-to resource for business and tennis courts. In other words, with Homer gone, the potential for chaos was very high. And he was only gone for two days before the god of chaos struck.

"Papa, can you please fix the toilet in the girl's room?" Mikhail asked pointedly.

"What? You are the butler, aren't you? You can do it!" Vladimir was upset with Mikhail because the budding butler had turned his attention away from helping his father finish the tennis courts. But then again, Mikhail had new responsibilities and delegations. Valentina stayed out of their quarrel but reigned supreme in the kitchen. Her area of responsibility was under control until the dishwasher broke down and the sink backed up. Then she told Vladimir to fix it, to which he responded, "Call the plumber." The three adults broke down into a shouting match until Anya and Tanya showed up and directed the family's senior members to cease their feuding and act like adults—seek outside mediation if they couldn't get their act together. All this from twelve-year-old twins. Now there were five Agapovs feuding.

Before long, Ludmilla wandered into the kitchen where the feud had found a home and issued a proclamation. The air from the air conditioner smelled like fungus, and the machine needed to be inspected by health authorities or an air conditioning technician. She wasn't sure whose problem this was to address, but she wanted to ensure everyone knew her professional judgment as an infectious disease expert. The other five looked at Ludmilla with puzzlement, took note, and moved on. Sasha showed up crying that her toilet had overflowed. Sasha sheepishly admitted that the backing up problem had been going on for a while. Maybe a month? Sasha also confided that her old toys didn't flush down the toilet as quickly as they once did. She liked getting new toys, so flushing her old ones was a favorite pastime. Boris showed up just then to say that his toilet was overflowing upstairs, and when he tried the hallway toilet, it was overflowing as well. Vladimir looked at Mikhail with a mixture of horror and humor.

"Ok, head butler, what do we do now?"

Mikhail hesitated and then summoned all of his knowledge and experience, mainly that his dad had taught him. "Okay, the sewer here is on a septic tank that must be full of toys and has started backing up. It will need to be pumped. Papa, can you call the company to do that? Mama, you and I will look at the dishwasher, fix it, or let the plumber do that. You may not like it kids, but you need to clean up the bathrooms and mop the floors quickly. No odors can be left," Mikhail spoke calmly and with authority. The house had been cleaned, the tank pumped, and the plumbing checked and repaired by the end of the day. Mama instructed Sasha on the proper disposal of old toys into a box for the Goodwill store. Papa and Mikhail inspected the floor that had flooded, pulled back carpets and hardwood until they got to dryness, and were able to fix the subfloors where needed. New carpet and tile would come later. Everyone calmed down, dinner was served, and the kids went to bed after watching their nightly shows. Vladimir and Mikhail finished the immediate work on the floors and then went to the shop in the basement to put away the tools. Papa gave Mikhail a beer, and they drank together in silent until they finally spoke to each other.

"Mikhail, you did very well organizing us today. You did a good job."

"Thank you, Papa. You taught me."

"Yes, but you took charge. That's not always easy to do under any circumstances but especially with your parents and family. I think you will make a fine butler."

"Papa, I was scared at first."

"Yes, it's understandable."

"But then I knew it was my responsibility to sort out who was doing what and to hold everyone accountable."

"Yes, and you did that well."

They talked for a little more about the specifics, then Vladimir wrapped his son up in a bear hug and said good night.

Mikhail inspected the bathrooms. Sasha's was dry, and the toilet flushed. He walked back through the main entry hall. The floor was dry with no foul smell. The toilet in the hallway flushed with no problem now. He inspected the ceiling on the first floor under the bathrooms for Sasha and Boris, and no water stains were found. Then, when he was satisfied that all was well, he went to the boys' bedroom. His brother was asleep. Michael laid down on his bed and thought about school and what things would be like when he returned. He needed to have that conversation with Mr. Homer when he returned from his sudden trip to Switzerland. Mikhail realized that he had only three weeks before he would depart for London and a new future.

Chilly fresh Swiss air and gorgeous sunshine poured in as Homer opened his eyes, glancing around his three-hundred-year-old bedroom. The room was filled with fine antiques and heirlooms. The ceilings, fourteen feet in height, displayed intricate plasterwork. Tall windows allowed sunlight to illuminate the fabrics and woods in the room, creating a soft glow. He eased out of bed and walked over to the window. Opening the windows wider, he could see the new day spilling out over the acres of vineyard with the Alps in the distance. Smells from the kitchen below declared the chef-prepared breakfast to come. Homer slipped on a housecoat and slippers that had been provided. He cautiously peeked out into the silent hallway and could hear voices downstairs. The Count had encouraged Homer the previous evening to wake early and come down to enjoy coffee. So Homer did. When Homer walked into the dining room, the Count was still in his pajamas and housecoat, like Homer. An attractive, slender, middle-aged woman with coiffed hair and a fashionable Italian dress sat across from the Count.

"Homer, please, sit here at the head of the table," as the ancient man patted his hand on the place setting. Homer obliged and made his way around to the head of the table. The woman stood and offered her hand.

"Monsieur Pitts, I am Heloise, the Count's personal attaché. I am pleased to meet you." Homer nodded politely.

"The pleasure is all mine," Homer responded. "Good morning, Papa." It was the first time he had tried it out, and it felt good. He said "Papa" in the French way, stretching out the last "pa." He was letting it linger for just a moment. The Count reciprocated with a sweet smile. "So, what is the schedule for today?"

"Two activities after breakfast," the Count said. "A trip to my bank in Geneva, first. Then the rest of the day will be spent at the lake house. We will take a boat from the lake house to Geneva. That will be an enjoyable ride. It is the only way to travel around the lake as far as I am concerned," the Count said.

"Splendid," Homer replied as the butler filled his cup with freshly brewed coffee. Cream and sugar were added, and Homer took a little fruit and a croissant to eat. The conversation continued light and warm, like the air coming in through the French doors open to the patio. Their breakfast lingered for an hour or so with no rush. Heloise left after twenty minutes, and the remainder of the time the Count and Homer spent talking about the lakehouse. The Count was catching up on Homer's education and life in New York and his travels to Paris and Milan years before. They discussed what Homer had done since his mother passed away. The Count probed Homer's plans and the likelihood that he might relocate someday to live a more urban and civilized existence. Homer responded with a firm no to moving, but instead, he was interested in bringing civilization to his rural home. The Count respected Homer's intentions. For Homer to relocate at this stage of life would be like asking the Count to relocate from his beloved Switzerland in these his last years. He enjoyed London and the other cities where he had lived, but the Count always wanted to come home. Homer and the Count were kindred spirits where their homes and their roots were concerned. They finished the breakfast, and then both went to their rooms for showers. They also realized that both of them were compulsive twice-a-day shower-takers. At bedtime and first thing in the morning. Showers—not baths.

By mid-morning, the two men and their entourage left the estate and headed to Hermance, where the lake house was. A half an hour later, the Mercedes carrying them pulled onto a crushed gravel drive and down through giant cedars toward the sparkling blue water of Lake Geneva. As they emerged from the cordon of trees, a modern, three-story stone and glass home came into view, with large slate patios, flowers, a pool, and an elevated, spectacular view of the lake. The driver pulled the car into a garage attached to the home. The live-in housekeeper and gardener met the Count at the door. On entering the house, Homer could see a panoramic, unobstructed view of the lake through the two-story, floor-to-ceiling windows ahead. A broad patio extended beyond the windows.

Homer could also see a boathouse at the water's edge and a vintage boat secured to the pier, a Riva Aquarama no less. Sleek, polished wood, and a powerful engine, the classic Italian powerboat was beautiful. After tea and biscuits and polite conversation to introduce Homer to the staff, the Count led Homer, a helmsman, the gardener, and a security agent down to the boat. As Homer got closer, he could see that this was a Lamborghini model Riva Aquarama from the late sixties. Those models were outfitted with two V12 Lamborghini engines and could go faster than fifty miles per hour. They got in, and the helmsman brought the boat roaring to life with a deep, bone-shaking rumble and then accelerated smoothly out into open water. The ride to Geneva was exhilarating, especially on a clear, crisp, windless day. At the pier in Geneva, a chauffeur met the party and drove the Count and Homer, along with an armed security agent, to downtown Geneva.

The Count's bank was located in a small, unassuming three-story building on a quiet back street. The two-hundred-year-old building had few external markings and no signs. The Count, Homer, and the others entered and were taken down a stairwell to a large room with comfortable chairs. The driver and security agent sat down and began reading the magazines lying on the coffee table. A bank agent came out and took the Count and Homer down a hall to a large room with no furnishings but with a wall of deposit boxes. Then, the men entered a smaller room that was completely bare except for a single box in the wall. The box had two keyholes and a handle. The Count inserted his key, and the bank manager inserted his. The manager turned the handle to open the box. Inside was a silver handle that looked ancient and worn. The bank manager pulled the handle, and a click could be heard deep inside the wall. A door in the wall opened, barely wide enough for a single person to enter, passing into an inner chamber. The Count walked in using a flashlight he had brought with him. The bank manager was next, and then Homer. Nothing was said amongst the men. Once inside, they walked twenty feet down a tunnel and came to another door.

The Count pulled out a large iron key and inserted it into the door. He turned the mechanism with an audible click. The door was heavy and yet, once pulled, it opened quickly. Only the Count and Homer entered. Once inside the next chamber, the Count found a light switch on the wall and flipped it on. Crackling loudly, an ancient set of fluorescent bulbs came on and cast light throughout the room. The sight Homer beheld left him stunned—a large room with about a hundred bags in rows in the middle. Around the edges of the room were various candlesticks, swords, pitchers, vases, and other items made of gold and silver. The bags in the middle were made of canvas material and appeared quite old. The Count walked up to one, untied the string holding the top closed, and reached in. He pulled out an object that shined in the light and appeared to be a coin.

"Homer, I will explain what this is when we are back at the house. For now, just know that what I am showing you is a gold coin from the reign of the Byzantine Roman Emperor Constantine IX. There are about one thousand coins in pristine condition in each bag. The coins here are from Constantinople. There are also coins minted for King Phillip of France—that evil man. The value of each coin ranges, but they average around $2,000 apiece. You and I are the only ones now who know about this. Even the bank manager never comes past that outer door. It's the St. Clare fortune that started with the bags of coins and then, over the next thousand years, enlarged. Conservatively, what you see here is worth at least a billion U.S. dollars." With the brief description, they exited the vault and headed up into the main building. Homer's mind was spinning. As they rode away from the bank and back to the marina, the men in the car were silent. The conversation resumed when Homer and the Count were alone at a Marina Café table for two by the water.

"You see, Homer, you are the bastard, illegitimate continuation of the thousand-year-old St. Clare line—terms to describe you that I despise. As far as I am concerned, you are my son and my only legitimate heir. But people who care about noble bloodlines don't care about what I believe. They care about who is married to whom and who that produces. They don't even necessarily care about when the marriage occurs."

"I think I understand. But nobility is something we don't have in the United States, you know."

"I know. But it is more about setting right for eternity what was not set right in life, wouldn't you say?"

Homer gulped. The words were a catchphrase he had used since childhood. It justified his persistence on the land issue with the town and many other lost causes he had pursued. He always thought he came up with it himself, but maybe not.

"But what does that have to do with your present situation, Papa."

"Everything. Being officially in the bloodline will make it easier for me to leave you the inheritance. And becoming a French citizen is also easier."

"French citizenship? I thought you were Swiss?"

"I am. But I served in the French Foreign Legion for five years when I was young before going to New York. I was able to claim dual citizenship—Swiss and French. And France is about the only country in the world where necrogamy is legal."

"Necrogamy?"

"Posthumous marriage."

"Excuse me, what?"

"Marriage where one of the parties is dead. You see, Homer, I want to marry your mother. I believe our letters reflect that, and as a French citizen, it is legal for me to marry her. I believe your mother's husband died before she did, so she was not married at the time of her death."

"That's right, but they divorced before he died."

"Even better for this situation."

"But why would you do this, Papa?"

"Two reasons. To strengthen my case to make you my official legal heir if some want to challenge it, and most importantly, because I loved your mother. I want to spend my eternity with her as my true wife."

"I see. Well, what would you need?"

"Her."

"She is dead."

"I know. Her remains, I mean. I know it sounds morbid, but if her remains come to France, we could marry, and then she could be interred in my family's mausoleum."

"Did you ever talk to her about this? She was insistent on being placed in a mausoleum back home."

The Count hesitated. He reached into his sweater pocket, pulled out a yellowed envelope with a letter, and handed it to Homer. Homer read it, quickly at first and then more slowly.

"So, she knew all this before she died. She knew you would continue to look for her and me."

"Yes. She could easily have told me where you were, but she wanted to ensure that my love for her was genuine. And I think she surmised that if I could ever find you both, even after she was dead, that that would be proof."

Homer sat speechless, pondering it all. He could understand her last words to him now. And he somehow knew deep in his soul that coming to France, marrying the Count at least in spirit, and spending her eternity next to him was what she would have wanted—however unlikely and bizarre it was.

"Papa, I will help you realize this wish. I believe it is the right thing to do."

Homer and the Count were quiet the remainder of the morning. They talked, swam in the pool at the lake house that afternoon, and enjoyed dinner together. A day of sightseeing in the Alps followed as well as a short trip to Basel. The entourage returned to the family estate and vineyard on Saturday night to a feast and fireworks. Sunday morning, Homer bid farewell to his newly found father.

"Papa, thank you for finding me."

"I think I owe that to Horatio, your llama."

"I will reward him when I get back. And you, could I entice you to come to Georgia?"

"Maybe, one day. But for now, I want to savor the time you and I have had. And to start planning for Angeline's trip."

"I understand." Homer leaned down and kissed his Papa on the cheek and gave him a gentle hug.

As Homer left, he turned around one last time and waved. He wasn't sure he would ever see his Papa again, alive. But he would make sure to follow through on the marriage.

The flight home seemed shorter than when he traveled to Switzerland. He was eager to return home even though his few days in Switzerland were life-changing, life-affirming. Mikhail was there at Hartsfield-Jackson to pick him up and take him home. During the forty-minute drive, Mikhail updated Homer on the estate's goings-on, the plumbing problems, what he had done to fix things, and the costs. Homer thought that Mikhail had matured a bit while he was gone. Mikhail confided to Homer that his father helped set him straight about what it would be like to be in charge. Homer nodded approval.

The limo eased into the estate around dusk. Homer headed inside as Mikhail got his bags. Vladimir welcomed Homer at the door, and Valentina had a charcuterie plate ready with a glass of cabernet sauvignon. Homer talked to the three of them about his trip; then, he excused himself for a shower and light reading. As Homer lay down on the bed, his final thoughts were of the Count. Views of his life and all he had seen and done—of his pain and agony—and the purse. The Count gave Homer a little gift-wrapped box to take back to America. When Homer settled in his bed at home, he looked in the gift, and Homer found one of the gold coins and two keys. And an old, leather book with a story that went back to Friday, October 13, 1307. It was the journal of Sir Artesius St. Clare, Templar Knight of Lyon.

CHAPTER 22

THE YEAR WAS 1307

The inscription on the first page of the old, worn leather book read "The Journal of Artesius." The writing in the book was in Old French, which Homer could translate reasonably well.

"I, Artesius, a Poor Fellow-Soldier of Christ and the Temple of Solomon write these words as a testament of my actions. I came from the Holy Land by way of Montpelier, leading a group that included two other knights who will remain unnamed for their protection in these perilous times. Our caravan included several coaches, wagons, sergeants, and pages carrying a treasure evacuated from a besieged castle in the East. We fought bravely to secure the prize and intended to transport it back to the Templar fortress in Lyon. As we traveled, a fortuitous stopover at a tavern near St. Etienne allowed us to overhear King Phillip's drunk local agent describe the king's treachery to arrest all Templars the next day, Friday the 13th. I was not naïve to the ways of treacherous men and had myself fought as saint and devil alike. On that night, I could see through the cloak of indifference in the tavern to understand that the Templar Knights would be exterminated for our treasure once arrested. I also realized that the King's soldiers could take the treasure from us at any time and execute us without repercussion. The Alps would offer some protection to the east, I thought. I could not convince my fellow Knights to depart, but they bid me no ill will in leaving. I took my portion of the treasure, one hundred bags of gold coins from the time of Justinian II, and departed into the night. I rode hard on a warhorse with two draft horses pulling a wagon carrying the gold coin, helmed by a young page who came with me. On the third day, we entered the Holy Roman Empire, steering clear of towns and any large gatherings of soldiers. Arriving on the fourth day near Geneva, we obtained some local farmer's trousers and tunics and then traveled for five more days until I reached Uri, where I deposited the coin in a hidden cave I knew about from years past. The page left me with a small bag of coins as his reward. I did not see him again, nor did I know his fate. I settled down in Geneva and gradually built both reputation and fortune, excelling at banking and statesmanship. I married and had children, two boys, and a girl. When the time came for war, I carefully advised the local farmers without revealing my time as a Templar. I used the gold sparingly and only when the investment would generate profit. Our family has prospered, and as I approach my eightieth year, I thank the Lord for sparing me, a humble servant, from the fate of so many." The signature was faded, but the author's name appeared to be "Artesius of Lyon."

From Artesius, forty generations of St. Clare's prospered in the Swiss Alps, building an enormous fortune with holdings worldwide. And it now would all come down to Homer to either continue the line or let it finally die out. He felt an unfamiliar weight and sense of responsibility settle on him as sleep finally arrived. Homer would decide how to proceed in a newly illumined and complicated world in the morning. Convinced that God, or fate, intervened in unpredictable ways to advance civilization, Homer's contemplated his place in it.

In the morning, Homer awoke, strengthened, and refreshed. And as he walked downstairs in his silk housecoat, scarf, and pajamas, Homer had no idea how different his life would be by the end of the day from this simple beginning. It would begin with an exciting update from Mikhail, just as Homer approached the dining room for breakfast.

And the first day of the rest of Homer's life would end with a petite, aesthetic woman named Emilia Gisler.

CHAPTER 23

ARCHAEOLOGY IN GRACE

While Homer was away, the Grace Historical Society added an essential new member. Major Lowman started the recruitment with a simple phone call the morning before Homer returned.

"The Grace History Center needs a part-time archaeologist to help us with a dig on the Homer Pitts property. Would you be interested?" Major Lowman was direct with Contessa Teabody. She didn't know whether to be offended or flattered. Her credentials were world-class, and the reason she lived in Grace was Alvin. She would have been more at home in Boston or New York or London. Candidly, she thought the ridiculous idea to turn a four-person fistfight into a Civil War monument and battlefield as part of a castle complex was farcical. But she was sort of flattered that the local guys wanted her on their team. So, she chose to check her pride at the door and hear them out. She invited them to her house to discuss the proposal the following afternoon.

The team showed up at the Teabody residence around 4 p.m., with Alvin joining as well.

"Gentleman, welcome to our home," Contessa's beautiful smile conferred warmth and graciousness. "Let's sit at the dining table. I would like to hear a little more of your story." Major Lowman, former sheriff Meeks, the Reverend Jackson, and two recent recruits, Dr. Hippo and Dr. Youseff filed into the dining room and took seats as she opened the door. Contessa sat at the head of the table, and Alvin sat at the other end.

"Ma'am and Sir, we constitute the Grace Historical Society. We have been researching a battle that took place toward the end of the Civil War. The battle involved four men," Major Lowman said. Alvin smiled and dropped his head when he heard the number four. But Contessa was a scientist, and whether it was four or four thousand, she was always searching for new data, new ideas, and new theories. The Civil War was not specifically her area of interest, but she thought she could provide qualified primary archeological supervision.

"Yes, Major Lowman, I have heard about your goal. But what type of exploration are you planning? Are you going to do a dig, or are you conducting a record review? What about a broader exploration? We could sift some of the creek bed, I suspect. You would be surprised as to what might be found."

The major smiled. Contessa said, "we." That meant she was at least interested. The other guys got it too. For forty-five minutes, the unlikely group went over some of the possibilities. Even the new members, the medical doctors, added some essential concepts to the discussion. By the end of the conversation, the team agreed to meet with Homer the following afternoon. All in all, it was a good start. Alvin was smiling the whole time, thinking about what Homer would say when he heard their pitch.

ARCHAEOLOGY IN GRACE

▲

At Homer's estate the following day, Mikhail updated Homer as he entered for breakfast regarding the upcoming visit.

"Mister Homer, we did not tell you last evening that you will have some visitors today. A party of six from the Grace Historical Society is coming to solicit your participation and support of a new historical initiative in Grace," announced Mikhail with a new formality that he was adopting before he left for London in ten days.

"Grace Historical Society?" Homer asked as he buttered his croissant to compliment the ham and cheese omelet and orange juice he was having for breakfast. "I thought there was just a town historian, Major Lowman?"

"Sir, there is now a full society that includes the major along with the Reverend Jackson, former Sheriff Meeks, Dr. Hippo, Dr. Youseff, Dr. Teabody as a professional consultant, and her friend from Atlanta, Dr. Gisler. Emilia Gisler, I believe."

"I see—quite the illustrious group. This Dr. Gisler, do you know what kind of doctor she is?"

"I believe she is a Professor at a European university in the field of archaeology. She is visiting Dr. Teabody."

"And do you have any idea why these people are coming out here today?"

"They would like to excavate the Civil War battle site on the property," Mikhail said. Homer was confused because he did not know of a battle site on or near his property.

"Where is the site if I could be so bold as to ask?" Homer asked between bites of his omelet.

"In the creek, right where the little bridge is," Mikhail responded.

"I didn't know there was a battle there?"

"Four men had a fistfight and then stopped and rode to Tennessee together. Two were Confederates, and two were in the Union," Mikhail repeated what he had heard secondhand.

"And this battle? Does it have a name?" Homer asked.

"The Skirmish at Little Creek," Mikhail replied.

"I see. Interesting."

"They will be here around ten."

"Well then, I better go take a shower and dress appropriately."

"Yes, Mister Homer, I believe that would be in order."

"Mikhail, you are already growing into your role as a butler. Thank you."

"You are most welcome, sir."

Homer finished his breakfast and a few interesting articles in the New York Times. He read these on his iPad even though he preferred a physical paper. The actual paper was a day late, and the iPad was up to the present minute. So, he opted for the iPad. Quickly leaving the table, he headed to his bedroom to shower and dress. When he returned, he was in a proper mood to greet his guests, wearing a beige jacket and slacks and a navy blue-collared golf shirt. He went out on the patio with an iced latte prepared by Valentina. He could hear the front door chime ringing, but Mikhail would handle that and escort the group back to the patio. Homer rose and greeted Major Lowman when the group stepped onto the terrace and each of the other folks by name with a firm handshake. When he came to Dr. Gisler, he lingered for a moment, much to his surprise. They shook hands slowly and stared into each other's eyes for an uncomfortably long time.

ARCHAEOLOGY IN GRACE

▲

Emilia Gisler—a petite, unconventionally attractive French woman with a slight Italian accent came to Atlanta to study archaeology with world-famous Dr. Teabody. Dr. Gisler's spent her childhood in the comfortable confines of Monaco. At sixteen, she moved to Paris to live with her aunt while studying at the Sorbonne. After Paris, Emelia attended Oxford and met Contessa there. She spent time at Harvard as well and then moved on to Rome to study at the Vatican. Europeans' early explorations of North America and Central America were her specialty, particularly the early exploits of the English, Spanish, and French. She had a side interest in the Holy Roman Empire and a myth about the Templars escaping to America with treasure. She explained all of this as she and Homer talked. Homer regaled her with his knowledge of European history, particularly one tale of a Templar fortune having relocated to Switzerland, which she promptly acknowledged and then dismissed as unlikely. When they finally stopped talking, and without taking their eyes off each other, Mikhail politely intervened to invite everyone to be seated as he offered juices and coffee. The assembled group sat down and waited for Mikhail to return with drinks. Valentina also came with a basket of muffins she baked that morning.

Major Lowman spoke first.

"Mr. Pitts, we are interested in excavating the Little Creek at the Little Bridge to examine."

Homer jumped in. "To find evidence of a Little Battle, I hear." Homer smiled at his attempted humor, but the other folks looked at Homer with straight, unsmiling faces.

"Well, a Civil War battle, is that right?" Homer quickly added.

"Yes. A skirmish, or as you say, a little battle. But one that could be of significant historical interest," Dr. Teabody said.

"Doctors will lead our excavation. Teabody and Gisler, and the rest of us will assist in the clearing and searching," Major Lowman said to make sure that Homer knew this would be a very professional operation. "We estimate being onsite for three to five days, depending on our findings. Here are the permission forms and disclosures. According to the law, if any relics or valuable artifacts are found, those would be your property to do with what you want. We have taken the liberty of drafting a legal agreement that would state that fact and give us the right to photograph, test, and display any artifacts we find for a period of thirty days. Human or animal remains would be handled separately, and that is also spelled out in the agreement. We suggest that your lawyer review this with you before signing, and we are happy to discuss any concerns you might have."

"Okay, well, you came prepared, I see. I do have one question. You did say that any artifacts found on the property would still be mine, with the conditions you described, and that I could sell those artifacts if I so desired?" Homer was interested in this point.

"Homer, you can sell them, yes, but we are interested in the good that historical artifacts can bring to the public. We would love to have these curated and displayed in a museum if possible." Dr. Teabody was forceful and direct.

"I understand, Contessa, but I just want to make sure that I understand what I am and am not agreeing to in this transaction. I think it would be wonderful for Grace to have a bona fide archaeological exhibit, but I wouldn't want our artifacts shipped off to New York to sit in storage. Would you?"

"No," Contessa replied curtly.

"I would be delighted to host the Grace Historical Society in this excavation. Do you have a sponsor?"

"No, this is a voluntary effort," the major offered.

"Well, let me be the first to provide you some funding. How about $100,000 to start with?"

The group was stunned and speechless.

"Do you have a nonprofit foundation?"

"No," the major said.

"Well, let's set one up. Do you have a lawyer?"

"No, not really."

"How about I contact my lawyer and have him get in touch with you to set up the foundation? And I will be the first contributor. How is that?"

"A lot more than we expected."

"When can you start digging?"

The major looked at the other members of the group and then turned back to Homer.

"We can start Monday next week."

"Very good. We will welcome you back on Monday." Homer smiled at Dr. Gisler, who appeared to be favorably impressed with Homer's great interest, forcefulness, and generosity. In the dig, that is.

While Homer and the team discussed the archeological excavation, another group admired their handiwork in the yard. Jack, Vladimir, and Mikhail looked out over the three finished tennis courts with a sense of pride for what they had accomplished.

"Vladimir and Mikhail, good job. These courts look good, and it will be fun to play."

"Jack, you gave us the confidence and the help to get it done."

Vladimir lifted his racket and hit a tennis ball over the net of the first court.

Mikhail swung at the ball and missed. He had never played tennis. Vladimir hit a second tennis ball, and Mikhail cut again. Mikhail hit the ball the third time, and it sailed over the fence well out into the pasture.

"Mikhail, have you ever played tennis?" Jack asked.

"No," Mikhail answered honestly.

"Oh. Well, we need to add you to the school with Mr. Teabody," Jack said with a big grin.

"Jack, why don't you take the racket, and let's hit a few," Vladimir proposed.

Jack hadn't held a tennis racket in over twenty years, but his game came back to him very quickly. A few hard returns and Jack and Vladimir were playing for keeps. You would have believed it was Wimbledon the way the two men were challenging each other. Jack won the impromptu match, holding serve and winning five sets to four. In the end, Vladimir sprinted to the net to thank Jack and encourage him to play more. Alvin Teabody would come later in the afternoon to view the courts and test them further.

As the three men walked away from the courts and over to the main house, Homer came out to meet them and congratulate them on building the courts.

"Outstanding job, gentleman. The courts are first-rate!" Homer said.

"Yes, it's a real achievement, Mister Homer, one that we are proud of. But we couldn't have done it without Jack!"

"Well, I think that Mikhail and Vladimir deserve all the credit," Jack said.

"It was a group effort and group success!" Mikhail contributed.

"Don't get too relaxed, though, because we need to start working on the plans for the castle."

Jack winced. A castle would take six months to a year just to plan.

"Yes, Mister Homer, we are ready!" Vladimir's confidence was high and his enthusiasm strong. "But we can't build until Mikhail returns from his training. He has to be part of the plans."

Mikhail suddenly felt more pressure to return before he had even gone. Jack intervened.

"My best advice is to slow down, get some serious architectural input and draw out detailed plans before you even turn one spade of dirt. Otherwise, you risk a twenty-million-dollar mistake or two."

Homer recognized a voice of reason and couldn't afford mistakes, costly ones.

"Yes. I believe you are right, Jack. And Vladimir as well. Mikhail needs to be back before we start work."

Jack, Vladimir, and Mikhail all relaxed and breathed a sigh of relief.

CHAPTER 24

DR. EMILIA GISLER

The week went by quickly, and by the following Saturday, Homer needed a break. He had a secret plan to get a robust nap in his new rope hammock without interruption. His nightly sleep had been fitful lately, mainly because of dreams and a spell of nocturnal bear growling. To that end, Homer arranged for the Agapovs to go shopping in Atlanta for tennis clothes, followed by a dinner out at a popular Mexican restaurant, the El Maya. Before they left, the Agapovs all came to say "adios" to Mister Homer. Homer sat on the patio in his dark green robe, a pair of sandals he had had for ten years, khaki Bermuda shorts, and a blue and white polo shirt as all the Agapovs arrived to say "bye."

After getting a bunch of hugs, Homer finally waved them off. "Don't waste time, go, go to your shopping and eating extravaganza and have a great time," he said. The Agapovs obliged as they headed out for their afternoon on the town. Homer, alone at the mansion for once, headed back in to refill his sweet, iced tea before taking his little *siesta* out in the rope hammock hanging from the oak trees by the kitchen window. As he walked into the kitchen, he heard someone drive up. Homer looked out and saw Alvin, Contessa, and the interesting Dr. Gisler get out and begin walking to the door. He hadn't planned on having visitors this morning, so he hurriedly looked around the kitchen to find some sweets or crackers with cheese with which to entertain. But, the kitchen wasn't his domain, so Homer was empty-handed when the doorbell rang. He greeted them like long-lost pals, invited them into the kitchen, then quickly out onto the patio.

"Homer, we just came to see the tennis courts. Can't stay long," Alvin spoke up.

"Alvin, yes, that would be terrific, but can't you stay to have some refreshments!" Homer looked mainly at Dr. Gisler, smiling as he talked.

"Homer, while you two boys look at the courts, Emilia and I wanted to walk over to the creek and take a look around. We can figure out what we need to have to get a good start on Monday," Contessa said.

"Oh yes, Contessa, please do, and when Alvin and I are finished, we will come over and join you."

"Oh, we won't take long, Homer, just a few minutes," Contessa said while Emilia graciously smiled at Homer.

Alvin and Homer walked over to the courts. Alvin took out a tape measure and checked all of the line lengths as well as net heights. He walked all three courts, checking for unpredictable or uneven bounces from the tennis balls. He served a few from each service line. In ten minutes, he finished his assessment.

"Homer, your guys built perfect courts. I mean professional grade. Did they build courts before?"

"Not to my knowledge."

"Well, if they ever decide to go into business building them, they will get rich. These are professional-grade courts."

"Alvin, that's wonderful. I will tell them. Now, let's go over to check on the girls." Homer bolted toward the field where Contessa and Emilia were looking around. Alvin jogged to catch up with him.

"Homer, this creek is pretty rocky, and I think we will need to pull a lot of the rocks out to see if there are any artifacts underneath," Contessa informed Homer. "I am not sure there will be anything from the little battle the guys want to investigate, but I am interested in Native American artifacts as well. Some old documents and maps suggest that this pasture may have, at one time, been a relatively large Creek or Cherokee village—maybe even older. We aren't far from the Etowah Indian Mounds, New Echota, and a well known ancient rock wall. If the rest of the guys want to look for artifacts from the Civil War, fine, but Dr. Gisler and I are interested in much older history."

"Well, Contessa, that's music to my ears," Homer replied, already calculating that their interests might align with his plans to turn the estate into a historically significant visitor's destination.

"Yes, Mr. Pitts, I study ancient European civilization and am interested in the exploration that reached this area, particularly the Spanish from the south. DeSoto came through we know, and others may have as well," Dr. Gisler added.

"Well, I think you need to spend as much time as you can here, and I will be delighted as a host to make sure your expedition is successful. May I be so bold as to ask how much exploration or excavation you plan? And by the way, please call me Homer." He directed his intense gaze at Dr. Gisler.

"Well, there is about a forty-foot square area here," Contessa pointed to a bend in the creek where the relatively new footbridge had been built, "That looks interesting, and we may want to do some excavating around here."

"Well, don't hesitate to expand further. My land here is about 300 acres and extends up that hill," Homer pointed to the hill behind them, the mountain of his youthful explorations. "I believe there may be a cave or two up there. Certainly, there are plenty of stone markings and little walls that might be interesting, I suppose."

"Sounds promising," Dr. Gisler said, smiling. Homer smiled back.

"Well, we better go. We have to take Dr. Gisler back to her apartment in Atlanta," Alvin said as he tried to move the party back toward his car.

"Oh, Dr. Gisler, are you leaving our little town of Grace?" Homer was mortified.

"Just for the weekend. I have some work at the university that I need to complete so that I can enjoy my time here next week," Emelia replied.

"Wonderful." Homer was relieved.

CHAPTER 25

CHOOSING A NEW SHERIFF

Carl still had trouble with her name: Brunhild Dinsky. Simple in writing, not so simple in vocalizing. You had to have a very definite stop with one "d" and a gap of silence before you pronounced the second "d." If you didn't, then it ran together into one garbled mess that caused embarrassment. She was the last candidate for sheriff that Carl had to interview and probably the last person he wanted to see. Frankly, with the chaos she caused at the hospital, he couldn't believe that she made it through the preliminary interviews. Her resume was impressive, though. High honor high school student, Army Airborne Special Operations unit—the famed Night Stalkers, FBI, and recently, the Georgia Bureau. Several commendations and awards, private pilot license for both fixed-wing and rotary aircraft, and strong letters of recommendation. No disciplinary issues, no substance abuse issues, no supervisory issues, no personal issues. The model leader and, really, the Grace sheriff position was way below where she should be. And that was why Carl had to do the interview. He had to be tough and think this through. Because she was way overqualified and over-experienced to be in this position, Carl had to explore three things: 1) she had serious faults not recorded yet 2) she just wanted to live in a small town and would sacrifice to be there or 3) she was just passing through on to something better. He could live with 2 and 3 but didn't want to miss number 1 if that was the problem. He closed her file and asked his secretary to show her into his office.

When Officer Dinsky walked in, he had a visceral reaction in a good way. She was professional in appearance—dignified even. Despite her incredible height, her business suit was impeccable. Two-button black jacket, white blouse, black pants with heels. Attractive but not too much, and professional, yet relaxed. He would feel comfortable with her representing the city of Grace. As she approached, Carl reached out, and they shook hands. A firm but not overpowering grip. They sat down.

"Officer Dinsky, I am glad to see you again and appreciate your applying for the position here in Grace. This is the last interview, and I will be deciding in the next week," Carl said quickly, and Dinsky nodded that she understood.

"Let's start with why you want to be the sheriff in Grace?"

"To be or not to be, that is the question. I want to be a super cop in a town where I can grind the bad guys into the dirt. And I think Grace is exactly the place to put all my lethal training to work," she said in a steady, professional, pleasant way. Carl had no idea what she was talking about. This was by far the worst answer for any position for which Carl had ever interviewed anyone. It was so off that Carl became disoriented. How could everything she said and had done before lead to this? Or did he just imagine this answer?

"Okay, Officer Dinsky. Well, what are your goals if you do become the sheriff?"

"To ensure the safety of the residents of Grace, to support the growth and personal development of our officers, to build strong ties between the office and our community, and to wisely manage resources provided by the town." She answered this time with the same demeanor, but Carl thought it was better than the first answer.

"What's the toughest situation you have been in?" was Carl's next question. She vividly described a situation in Iraq where a position was about to be overrun by ISIS fighters. She had to evacuate a squad on the ground under withering gunfire. It was a gripping, splendid answer connecting the stress of that moment to situations relevant to a small-town sheriff.

Carl went on to ask a total of ten questions. The first one had been the worst, the other nine among the best he had ever heard. Well, 90% maybe wasn't so bad after all. He made the mistake of asking one more question.

"If you were to get this job, what would be your first act as sheriff?"

"Oh, that's easy. I would throw a big party and probably get drunk." Again, she answered with the same professional demeanor that she had with the other ten answers.

Carl thanked Officer Dinsky and saw her out of his office. He went back in, closed the door, and went to his desk. He wasn't sure what had just happened. She was the best candidate, and it wasn't close, but she had also given the worst two answers in an interview that he had ever heard. He wasn't sure what to do, so he decided to go home and talk it over with Lula Bell.

Carl arrived home, and he and Lula Bell had a quiet dinner out on the porch. As they cleared the table and Lula Bell took the plates in, Carl pulled out the file on Dinsky from his worn, leather briefcase. Lula Bell brought out a piece of pecan pie with one scoop of vanilla ice cream on top and a cup of decaffeinated Earl Grey tea and set it in front of Carl. She had the pie with no ice cream and a cup of Lady Earl Grey with caffeine. She needed the extra boost because she had plans to do some gardening out back after they finished as long as the evening light lasted.

"Lula Bell, Officer Dinsky is my final candidate for sheriff. She is the best so far."

"What about Jessup?" Lula Bell asked.

"You didn't hear. Won the Georgia Lottery. He is officially a millionaire now. During his interview, he got so nervous we had to stop the interview twice to let him go outside and chew some nicotine gum. Somehow that calms him down. Go figure. I think the second time, he may have started lighting up again—poor guy. When I asked about his life ambitions, he wanted to play video games and collect Hot Wheels cars. Although he is our second strongest candidate, we both agreed that winning the lottery relieved any financial concerns he had and that it was time for him to ride off into the sunset and collect Hot Wheels full time."

"Oh. Isn't Dinsky the crazy lady at the hospital who thought we had a terrorist attack?"

"The same. She has an impeccable record on paper, but her insight and judgment leave me a bit nervous."

"I would say so," Lula Bell added.

CHOOSING A NEW SHERIFF

"I asked her why she wanted to be sheriff. She quoted Shakespeare, 'To be or not be? I want to be' is what she said. Well, she said more, but that was the high point. Toward the end of the interview, I asked her what her first act would be if chosen to be sheriff. She said, 'throw a party and get drunk.' Yet, her other nine answers were pretty much perfect."

"Are you asking my advice or just telling me?" Lula Bell wanted to make sure she knew her role in this conversation before she said anything. If Carl didn't want her advice, she was generally supportive or non-committal. But Lula Bell usually had strong opinions, so she gave it to him unvarnished if he wanted her advice. This little nuance of knowing your role was what had kept them together for the last nearly forty years.

"Advice."

"Hire her. She is no different than most men. Nine out of ten times, they are fine, but once in a while, they royally screw up. You included. If she is that good otherwise, then hire her with some controls in place."

"Like what?"

"She has to see you as her mentor and guide, and she has to bring important things to you for advice, not approval before she goes forward. Hopefully, you catch the crazy stuff before it happens. When crazy stuff does happen, well, that's more difficult. But you can call those a "low blood sugar moment" as long as they are infrequent, and nobody checks her blood sugar."

"Okay. Got it. Nice. I like the way you framed it. You should be mayor."

"I know. I should. But I don't want the hassle. Besides, I get to live on the mayor's outstanding salary and benefits without having the headaches."

Carl smiled at Lula Bell's sarcasm. It was delivered in that same dry, monotone voice without inflection or emotion that made him smile forty years ago and always warmed his heart.

CHAPTER 26

A VISIT TO THE CAVE

Homer slept fitfully. He had so many things swirling in his mind that he couldn't sleep. He finally snoozed off around 3 a.m. Then, at 4:30 a.m., Homer awoke, soaked in sweat with a vivid, powerful sense that he was not alone. He felt Gabriel's presence. And just before he awoke, he had heard Gabriel's voice again, like the last four decades, calling him. Homer just knew that Gabriel must have crawled into that cave, found some way to squeeze through the hole in the back, and fallen to his death. But none of the adults ever believed him. But now, Gabriel's voice called out to him more loudly and urgently than before. Homer had to go. But he couldn't go alone. The only person he could think of to go with him was Mikhail. Homer crept down the hall to the boy's room and eased in. Mikhail was sleeping soundly with a light snore, but Homer gently woke him. They quietly eased out of the room as Mikhail grabbed some clothes. Homer motioned for Mikhail to follow and then headed to the storage room in the garage. Once out of earshot of all the bedrooms, Homer leveled with Mikhail.

"Mikhail, I am about to ask you to do something that is well beyond anything I should ask. Especially with you leaving for London in less than 12 hours. But I just had a nightmare, and I need your help. We have to go spelunking."

Mikhail would be leaving for Hartsfield-Jackson Airport at noon to make a late afternoon flight. The whole family stayed up late telling stories, singing, and toasting Mikhail on his big adventure. With an impressive application followed by a phone call from Mr. Homer, Mikhail was accepted to the London Butler Training School without difficulty. Homer paid the tuition, travel, and living expenses after a lengthy discussion initiated by Mikhail about his future. Mikhail did his homework and was well prepared. Mikhail and Homer got clear about Mikhail's role, authority, and relationship to assure he would have the best chances to become an excellent butler. Two things were added to the deal. Homer secured an apprenticeship in a billionaire's household in Geneva, Switzerland, and agreed to give Mikhail a small acreage on the estate in Grace for when he returned. Mikhail would use the property to build a new house in which he would live. It would be on a distant part of the estate to provide some separation from the family. Homer and Mikhail were both happy with their arrangement after some tense negotiation. To accomplish his successful negotiation, Mikhail got advice from Carl, watched several YouTube videos on negotiating, and practiced with everyone he could before tangling with Mister Homer. Mikhail would carry that diligence with him into his butlership. And they agreed that when Mikhail returned, he would address Homer as "Master Homer" since Homer was the Master of the house, and Homer would address Mikhail as "Mr. Agapov."

Mikhail wasn't quite sure what to say about Homer's wee hour request. But as a butler, he just needed to accommodate the request.

A VISIT TO THE CAVE

▲

What was missing from the appeal was why at 4:30 in the morning, Homer needed Mikhail to help him climb into the cave to find Gabriel after four decades.

But it was Mikhail's job. So, together they gathered up flashlights, a shovel, an ax, hedge clippers, a rope, and a tiki torch that still had some kerosene in the can, along with a lighter, and headed out. It took them fifteen minutes to walk the pasture and make it to the cave covered by bushes and vines. About ten minutes to clear that away and then it took Homer five minutes to muster the courage to enter a place he had not entered in a long time. He squeezed through the opening and found himself in the familiar inner cavern. But Mikhail was too big to get in. Homer felt safer with Mikhail close by, so he told Mikhail to stay put.

Homer lit the tiki torch, and light filled the cavern. The many mice and rats scurried around in the light, which caused Homer to nearly have a stroke and dance a little jig to avoid stepping on them. But now, in the shadows deeper in the cave, there was something quite different moving. Larger and slithery. A fat, six-foot-long black rat snake sat curled up right in front of the tiny opening that led deeper into the cave where Homer needed to go. Homer felt his heart stop for a moment, then speed up. He wanted to run, but he couldn't. He was frozen. He used the shovel to prod the beast out of the way from afar but to no avail. It was too heavy for Homer to move. He reached down to pick up a rock to throw at the snake, but just as he touched it, the furry little rock moved. Homer winced as he wet himself when he realized the rock was a giant field rat nibbling on his boot. Luckily, the snake caught sight of something smaller than

Homer and eased out of the gap a little. But then it stopped. Homer feared nothing in this life like snakes, and he wasn't going to try to move further in with the snake in the way. He called out to Mikhail.

"Mikhail, there is a giant snake in here. An Anaconda, I fear! I need you to squeeze in with that ax or the hedge clippers and get him."

"Can I hand them to you, Mr. Homer?"

"No, you have to get in here."

Mikhail sucked in his stomach as flat as he could stand and stuck in, first, one leg, then his torso, and then his other leg. He was scraping the skin off exposed areas as he went. He had to bend at the waist and pull his upper body in last. And when he was finally in the cavern, he couldn't stand fully erect. But at least he was by Mr. Homer's side.

"Mister Homer, I see the snake. It is not a venomous snake."

"It's a snake, Mikhail. I hate, hate, hate snakes."

"Probably your upbringing, Mr. Homer. Garden of Eden, Satan and all that."

"Whatever. But kill the thing, please!"

"No. I will catch it."

Homer nearly fainted as Mikhail lunged, grabbed the twisting and writhing monster, and then pulled himself back through the opening while passing in front of Homer's face with the snake. When Mikhail was outside, Homer edged closer to the small space in the back of the cave. He remembered the sound of running water that you heard as you got closer. He and Gabriel had never been able to see very far down and were too scared to push in through the opening very far forward for fear of falling into the unseen water. Homer pointed the powerful industrial-strength flashlight beam back and down and could see now that there was a twenty-foot drop to a pool from the edge ahead. Maybe poor Gabriel had come here by himself and had fallen in all those years ago. Homer edged forward closer to the dark abyss. Before he got too far, he tied the rope around his waist in case he too slipped to his death. At least they would be able to pull his body out and give him a proper burial. Mikhail had thrown the snake out into the forest and then squeezed back into the cave. He stood directly behind Homer now, holding the other end of the thick rope.

"Mikhail, hold onto the rope for dear life, and I will scoot up as far as I can and look down in there to see if I can see what I need to see."

"Yes, Mister Homer," Mikhail answered. As a butler, he would not question the logic or sanity of his boss's actions, only be there to help him get the job done. But he did think this was a bit crazy.

"Okay, here I go," Homer said as he leaned forward. His footing was pretty good until he got near the edge, where he began to slip and then plunged about six feet. Homer dangled with his body perpendicular in an open space, staring down another twenty feet to the bottom of the cavern. Somehow, he still had the powerful light in his hands, and he shined it down into the pool of water at the bottom of the little waterfall. The water was crystal clear. Homer could see the unmistakable skeleton of what was, most likely, a little twelve-year-old boy. Homer began to sob uncontrollably—not from fright or pain—but the intense emotion that he had finally found his friend, Gabriel. He called Mikhail to pull him up. They gathered their supplies and squeezed back out of the cave into the early morning darkness. Though he was wet, bruised, and muddy, Homer felt some resolution to a pain that had never left him, and Mikhail felt a sense of accomplishment in serving Mister Homer with an unusual task.

When Homer awoke again, the rain was coming down outside as if the tears of heaven had finally been released. And the Agapovs were gathered to see Mikhail off. Homer hurried to get dressed and made it into the kitchen just before the entourage headed out to the car that would take Mikhail to Hartsfield-Jackson airport for his early afternoon flight to London. Officer Dinsky agreed to drive Mikhail to the airport and waited impatiently by her patrol car with an umbrella and a nervous smile. As Brunhilde's initial meeting with Mikhail's family since the bioterrorist attack, Mikhail reassured her that she didn't have to speak to them on this visit. It was more like reconnaissance.

Vladimir and Valentina were dripping tears as they hugged their eldest child before his journey out into the world. All the brothers and sisters hugged Mikhail, some superficially, wishing they too were escaping and others with tears and emotion because their big brother was leaving.

"Mikhail, where did you get all those scrapes and cuts?" Ludmilla asked with curiosity. She was perturbed about the risk for *Staphylococcal* skin infection, a bug she had just learned about this week.

"Oh, just doing some clearing out in the woods. No big deal." He answered calmly as his eyes met Homer's. Homer gave Mikhail some words of encouragement and hugged him, whispering a thank you to him for his help in the wee hours of darkness before dawn. As he embraced Mikhail and whispered thanks, Homer also slipped several hundred-dollar bills into Mikhail's coat pocket for spending money

A VISIT TO THE CAVE

▲

while he was away. And then it was finally time to go. Mikhail waved to the family and Homer and jumped into the soon-to-be sheriff's car. Officer Dinsky did her part by spinning the wheels in the driveway, spewing gravel everywhere, then squealing the tires as they pulled out onto the highway. She was very eager to leave, probably sensing the need to get to the airport early on a rainy day. Mikhail's embracing and hugging of her as they drove away was also probably his gracious thanks for her sacrifice of taking him to the airport on the morning of her big public announcement. But Valentina couldn't quite understand why he was taking off his shirt while they sped down the highway. She waved goodbye to him until they were out of sight. Valentina was so grateful that her boy was on the way to becoming a man!

Ludmilla pondered whether her big brother might be at risk for fungal infection like *Blastomycosis*. She decided she needed to go into the woods and get some samples up on the mountain where the woods were. She was just glad her big brother didn't go into the cave up there. There are all kinds of awful microorganisms in caves!

As the emotional send-off for Mikhail broke up and the Agapovs went about their chores, Homer's mood darkened, and he became somber. He now had to deal with Gabriel. He went to his office, closed the door, and called Carl.

"Carl, I know you have a lot going on this morning, but I have some very tragic news to share. I will make it short. I believe I have found Gabriel Montcliff's remains here on the property. Just this morning." Homer began to sob quietly as the tragedy and finality of what he just told Carl sank in.

"Homer, oh no. That poor little boy. I know you two were close friends back then, and I know Lula Bell will be heartbroken, as I am sure you are. She liked that boy. And Alvin, have you told him?"

"No, Carl. Just found him this morning. I won't go into all the details. Normally I would call the sheriff because we need the coroner to come, I guess. But with the changeover, I thought I would call you first."

"Thanks, Homer. I will take care of it. I know this is tough for you, but where did you find him?"

"In the cave. I always knew Gabriel was there. I had a nightmare last night about it that was just so strong I had to do something. It was like he was crying out to me. Mikhail helped me find him. Mikhail did a real good job helping me. Gabriel's remains are in a pool of water under a waterfall. It's going to be very difficult to get to them, I am afraid."

"Okay. Well, I will call the coroner and tell him he will need some expert help in that cave to get to little Gabriel."

"Yes. The coroner will need some real search and rescue types to get to Gabriel."

"Okay. Probably be this afternoon. Do you want to talk to the Montcliffs once we know?"

"Yes, I could do that," Homer said. "The last time I talked to them was when I bought the estate. It was a nice conversation, particularly with Mrs. Montcliff. I think the Montcliffs should know that even though they left a long time ago and live way down in Naples, that all of Grace remembers and still supports them at a time like this."

"Well said, Homer. Well said." Carl hung up and called the coroner. They decided to get a local spelunker with search and rescue

A VISIT TO THE CAVE

▲

experience down from Chattanooga. He would come out to the cave later in the afternoon.

Homer sat back as he finished the call and cried. Not a little sob but a full-throated, horrible cry that comes as a release after so many years of pain. He had a picture of Gabriel on his bookshelf from school. Old, black and white, and faded. He cried enough so that Valentina came to the door, almost knocked, but then didn't. She just listened and waited until the cry softened, and only little sobs could be heard. She knocked then.

"Mister Homer, are you okay?"

"Yes, Valentina. I will be out in a few minutes, honey."

Valentina went back to the kitchen and searched in the cabinet. She had several different types of honey, being that honey was an integral part of Russian cuisine. She found the best one. It was Siberian honey that her sister sent her three weeks earlier. Real Siberian honey from buckwheat and wildflowers. She put it on a little tray with a wooden spoon and some tea biscuits she made and took it back to Homer's office, knocking again on the door.

"Mister Homer, I have your honey. It's the real Siberian honey that my sister, Katya, sent me. You will like it very much. Would you like tea too?"

She could hear Homer get up from his chair and walk over to the door. He opened it. His face was reddened, and his eyes puffy and watery. His hair was disheveled as if he had been tearing at what little was there.

"Thank you, dear. Thank you. I love you and all of your family." Homer reached up and kissed Valentina on the forehead and her cheek. Then he straightened up, walked by her to the kitchen, and directed the family to prepare for the day. All while she stood with the honey on a tray. Mister Homer must not like Siberian honey, she thought.

Valentina went back and put the tray down on the kitchen counter and then shepherded the girls back to their rooms to get ready for the tennis training that would commence later. Alvin told the Agapovs to expect very intensive training during the whole first week—sort of like military boot camp. He felt the rain might be conducive to the kind of agony he expected to inflict on them this week to make them tough. His protocol required them to be athletes first and tennis players second, at least as they started. Valentina bought a few things for the girls while shopping in Atlanta on their little trip the day before. She laid the new sweatpants and T-shirts on their beds along with the latest tennis shoes, caps, shorts, matching towels and headbands, and new tennis rackets that Alvin recommended. The bill was pretty big, but her girls would be the best-outfitted tennis players around if Valentina had her way. Anya, Tanya, Masha, Ekaterina, Sonya, and Sasha thought they were all up to the challenge of becoming the premier tennis players in Grace.

CHAPTER 27

▲

MORNING IN GRACE

The rain eased off around 9:30 a.m., and the clouds parted, revealing a blue sky. Sunlight filtered through and began to dry the tennis courts. Alvin rolled into the driveway at 9:45. He unloaded his equipment and headed out to the tennis courts. With Alvin leading the way, Valentina and Vladimir walked to the courts carrying a water cooler and an ice chest full of grapefruit juice, orange juice, and ice. The girls trailed behind, appearing a little anxious about what was about to happen. The girls lined up on the tennis court at the middle court's service line when they arrived. Alvin gave them a quick rundown of the day to come and then had the girls run out into the field and around the edge of four times. One lap was ¾ of a mile, so four laps would be three miles. While they were running their laps, Alvin marked off a few places on the courts with tape. These markings would be for speed drills.

Alvin also had the girls running with a tennis ball in their left hands and a tennis racket in their right hands. Homer, Vladimir, and Valentina sat down in the kitchen for coffee and a quick, peaceful breakfast. Valentina had already been hard at work with homemade bread in the oven, the washing machine on spin cycle, the dishwasher starting a second rinse, and the downstairs vacuumed. Valentina greeted the busy day ahead with humming, singing, periodic prayers of thanks, and smiles in her few moments of peace. Vladimir went out with Boris and Ludmilla to feed the domesticated animals and the semi-wild deer. Afterward, Ludmilla went to the creek to collect a water sample so she could assess for bacteria. She wanted to be ready and know what she was fighting if all the archeologists developed dysentery later in the day.

The archeologists arrived around ten as Homer was leaving to attend the sheriff's announcement at Courthouse Square. The excavation team poured out of their minivan and unloaded shovels, rakes, buckets, spades, and plastic bags. As they did, Homer walked out to greet everyone. Contessa stepped forward first.

"Homer, how are you? I see Alvin already made it. Well, we are looking forward to a successful excavation this week."

Homer gave Contessa a little peck on the cheek. She was a strong, beautiful woman with hands that showed that she spent a lot of time doing manual labor. She had on a pink polo shirt and khaki shorts that hit just above her knees. Ankle-high boots and thick wool socks completed the outfit of a working archeologist. The two medical doctors, Dr. Hippo and Dr. Youseff popped around from the back of the van to shake Homer's hand and to thank him.

"Mr. Homer, I must say that you have a beautiful, grand estate here," Dr. Hippo commented. "Very much like my friends, the Ezes in Lagos, my hometown. Theirs is bigger, but your estate reminds me of theirs!"

"I second my esteemed colleague's observations on your property, Mr. Homer. I do think that your estate is wonderful and reminds me of my friends, the Mansours and the Sawiris. Theirs are larger and more opulent, but yours is reminiscent," Dr. Youssef added.

"Thank you both for your kind comments," Homer responded graciously.

Then there was the threesome: Major Lowman, former Sheriff Meeks, and Reverend Jackson. They came forward and shook Homer's hand as well. The men looked tired and a bit haggard. Homer hoped they had not been staying up late working on the dig and agonizing over plans to create the historical site. The men just wished they could kick the mushroom habit they had fallen into.

Dr. Gisler was the last person out of the van and yet the one person who Homer was particularly interested in seeing. She dressed in a black sleeveless blouse, khaki cargo pants, ankle-high boots and wore a seductive smile as she approached Homer. Her long black hair was in a ponytail hanging over her shoulder onto her chest.

"Good morning, Mr. Pitts. I hope you are well, although it looks as if you didn't get enough sleep last night. Are you okay?" Dr. Gisler asked.

"You're right. I did have a fretful night. But I am okay now. Thank you for asking," Homer responded, noting that Dr. Gisler was perceptive.

After a brief conversation, the group walked into the field and went to work.

Homer watched the entourage walk out to the dig site. Well, mostly, Homer watched Dr. Gisler. Glancing at his watch, Homer realized he was running late for the sheriff's announcement, so he jumped in his 1990 Porsche 944 Cabriolet and sped out along with

Vladimir in the passenger seat. Making it to Courthouse Square just in time, he and Vladimir joined the now restless crowd waiting for the announcement of the new sheriff.

Carl was on the hot seat as the master of ceremony for the announcement of the new sheriff. The rain had stopped, and Carl figured there was a forty-five-minute window for the event before the next gully washer hit. The new sheriff had not yet arrived, though. And Mikhail was late to the airport and in danger of missing his flight. No one at the square connected the two except for Homer. He didn't dare announce that the new sheriff left with Mikhail to go to the Hartsfield-Jackson airport over four hours earlier—a trip that should have taken her just two and ½ hours round trip.

With the announcement delayed until she arrived, Carl used the extra time to talk to Homer about a sensitive topic.

"Homer, I'm feeling old," Carl said.

"Carl, you are old," Homer replied.

"But, Homer, I don't like feeling old."

"Who does?"

"Well, I think after nearly forty years, it's time for me to step down from being mayor. That would free me up to play more golf, which makes me feel young."

"Carl, it's the Old Fashioned you have at the Country club bar after you play a round of golf that makes you feel young. Not the golf itself. You do know that, right?"

"Well, whatever. But at least I would be able to go out there every day instead of every other day. A 100% increase in treatment the way I see it."

"When are you going to step down? The election isn't for three years."

MORNING IN GRACE

"When I find somebody to take over. I don't have an assistant mayor, you know."

"How about Lula Bell's second cousin out at the hospital?"

"Betty Gilroy? Now that's an idea. She is close to retirement, I think. She has lived in Grace for most of her life. Served on the town council about twenty years ago. She was highly effective, but she was raising her kids and working and didn't have time for the council. So, she eventually rotated off. Nice lady, nice family. And she is no-nonsense. She doesn't put up with whining."

Homer was a champion whiner, so the thought gave him pause. "What do you mean, she doesn't put up with whining?" he asked.

Carl decided to take the bull by the horns. He looked at Homer. "Well, let's put it this way. Be glad you got your street named already."

"Oh. Well," Homer muttered.

"Yep. She could do it. I need to give her a call. Now, where is Dinsky?" Carl replied and started walking up to the podium.

Just then, Dinsky pulled into the Sheriff's parking space. She got out of the patrol car quickly and headed up to the stage. She appeared neither disheveled nor nervous, even though she and Mikhail made it to the airport barely in time for him to make his flight. A lingering kiss when she dropped him off was still fresh in her mind and her heart. They were in love and then she had to say goodbye to him for six months. Where they spent the missing two hours would be their little secret. When Dinsky dropped Mikhail off, she pulled away from the airport and hit the interstate with sirens and blue lights blazing. Over a hundred miles an hour got her up the interstate fast enough to make the announcement just fifteen minutes late. As she bounded up the stairs to the podium with evident energy and enthusiasm, Carl pointed to the chair reserved for her, and she sat down. He opened the ceremony with a short statement on the importance of the sheriff and the competitive process to arrive at a choice. Carl also commented on the high quality of the candidates and the outstanding credentials of the new sheriff. Then he announced her name.

"Let's welcome our new sheriff, Sheriff Brunhilde Dinsky," he said, leaving a pause between the end of her first name and the beginning of her last name to make sure it was clear. The applause was polite as the towering, gargantuan Sheriff Dinsky walked to the podium. An audible gasp came from the audience as they beheld her at full height.

"Thank you. I am honored to serve you, the people of Grace, in this new role. I will work every day to ensure that you are safe, protected, and included in the activities and policies of your Grace Sheriff's Department." The polite applause became a little louder.

"I look forward to ensuring that our force is the most professional and best-trained that it can be and that resources are used wisely and efficiently," she said, again with rising applause. She was on a roll. Nice place to say thank you and step aside.

"And I want to assure everyone here that no terrorist will find a haven here in Grace, that we will search out and destroy anyone who is a terrorist here or who supports terrorists." Dinsky voice grew bolder and louder.

Carl knew the sign and stepped in between Dinsky and the microphone.

"Thank you, Sheriff-designate Dinsky. I want to administer the oath of office now."

Carl proceeded to read the oath quickly, and as soon as Dinsky said, "Yes, I do," he turned to the crowd, thanked them, bid them safe travels, and turned off the microphone.

"Okay, well, welcome aboard, Sheriff Dinsky," he said, turning to her as she stood waving to the thinning crowd.

"Thank you, Mayor Longfellow. Sorry I was late, but I was seeing my future husband off at the airport," Dinsky said with a smile.

"Oh. I didn't know you were getting married?" Carl asked.

"He doesn't know either. But I will tell him when he gets back."

"Can you share who the lucky guy is?" Carl inquired.

"Mikhail Agapov-Pitts. He is so yummy," Dinsky shared with obvious delight.

Carl felt a little queasy and was concerned that the conversation was quickly drifting into "too much information" territory.

"Wow, just a while ago, we were just so . . ." Carl stopped her mid-sentence before images were shared that would be hard to wipe from his imagination.

"Sheriff, I have to go, but you call me if you have any questions. Have you decided about your force yet? Particularly Deputy Jessup?" Carl yelled as he walked quickly away.

"I'm meeting with him after lunch. Don't know whether to fire him or hire him."

"Well, he has been a regular part of the force, albeit rather ineffective. But it's your choice now. So good luck, and let me know if you have any questions. You know he won a big lottery prize, so I think he is probably ready to retire. You might take advantage of that. But it's your decision."

"Okay, Mayor!" Dinsky replied.

Carl headed quickly out into the remaining crowd to try to find Betty Gilroy.

As soon as the sheriff's announcement ended, Vladimir and Homer left for home. Usually, Homer would stick around and talk to the sheriff, Carl, and some other people from Grace who attended these gatherings. Mostly retired or unemployed folks with nothing much to do. It was always a good time to catch up. But today, Homer was on a mission to get back out to the house to see if Dr. Gisler would have a nice, pleasant lunch with him. He was worried that the lunch hour was probably almost over, and he might miss his opportunity. But maybe some tea and dessert would entice Dr. Gisler to take a break.

"Nice ceremony, don't you think, Mister Homer?"

"Yes, Vladimir. Quite nice, except why was she late?" Homer asked, already suspecting the real reason.

"I guess the traffic was bad when she took Mikhail to the airport," Vladimir said innocently.

"Maybe. Well, we have a new sheriff now, and Mikhail is on his way to London. What a day."

"Yes, and the tennis lessons and the archeological dig. Exciting day."

The drive from Courthouse Square back home was only three miles and usually took about ten minutes. He arrived home at 12:45, so maybe dessert was still possible with Dr. Gisler, Homer thought. As he opened the sports car door to get out, he noticed lots of commotion in the backyard.

Horatio was chasing the girls. When the girls ran through the field during Alvin's training drills, the goats became unsettled and started running away from them. Horatio, being the goats' guard and champion, challenged the girls and started chasing them. Alvin was clapping because he thought the added challenge of having a llama chasing them would be good training for the girls until Horatio spotted Alvin and started chasing him as well. So, there was general chaos now on the first day of tennis training on the estate.

The tennis training excitement did not affect the archaeological dig, but the diggers had their own excitement. As Homer was trying to understand how Alvin and the girls would extricate themselves from being chased by Horatio and a herd of goats, the archeologists came running toward Homer, yelling, "We found it. Something unexpected and sensational." He was ecstatic as Dr. Gisler ran to the head of the crowd to get to Homer first.

She had seen something unusual sticking up from the ground. When she investigated it and dug it out a bit, she realized it was Mayan-style pottery, never previously found in Georgia. A little piece, but with just enough markings to indicate Mayan origin. By noon, the group had dug up a site just inside the woods that revealed a few more small, broken Mayan-style pottery pieces, a ceramic spoon, and a small piece of jewelry. Even more spectacular was a near-pristine Spanish coin they found mixed with the pottery. Homer's land had suddenly become incredibly interesting with the potential to possibly yield some major artifacts from what appeared to be Mayans and Spanish explorers. In the space of just two hours, the site had become a place where both Dr. Teabody and Dr. Gisler wanted to spend a lot of time in the next few months.

Vladimir, who had been cleaning up leaves from the tennis court from the rainstorm that morning, wandered over to see what everyone was looking at. Homer, Contessa, and Dr. Gisler smiled at Vladimir and showed him the tiny bits of archeological treasure. Vladimir did not seem to be impressed.

"That little stuff. Not worth much, I think. Mikhail and I have been cleaning that stuff out when we built the courts. Just gets in the way." He was dismissive.

"Vladimir, what are you talking about?" Homer asked carefully.

"Just throw it out. That's what I say."

"Have you seen these kinds of things before?"

"Oh, yes. Mikhail and I have three whole baskets full. I kept finding this stuff when we were building the courts. Irritating and slowed us down."

Homer, Contessa, and Dr. Gisler froze. Homer spoke first.

"Can you show us where?"

"Oh, yes. Right back here." Vladimir led the group to the back of the nearby workshop. There against the workshop wall were three large wicker baskets that contained large whole pots, plates, tarnished silver jewelry, and a broad range of artifacts.

"This stuff just seemed like junk to me. Now we did find this stuff that I thought you might want to take a look at. Not sure what kind of money it is, though."

Vladimir pulled out an old blue Maxwell House coffee can, the Master Blend, and pulled off the plastic lid. Inside were around one hundred Spanish gold coins, most likely from the late 1600s, covered in dirt but in surprisingly good condition.

MORNING IN GRACE

▲

Dr. Gisler stopped cold. Her long, beautiful black hair tussled down around her neck as sweat glistened on her forehead. In the excitement, her heaving bosom mesmerized poor Homer as he stared at her with a half-smile, not knowing whether to turn away or grab her to join in the celebration. Contessa was more direct.

"This may be the greatest treasure ever found around here. Oh my God!" Contessa said.

Vladimir just shrugged. It just looked like old dishes to him.

By early afternoon, Valentina had prepared an excellent spread for lunch outside. The coroner and spelunker came and reclaimed Gabriel's bones in a discreet and honorable way. When the spelunker made it to his final resting site in the pool at the bottom of the cave waterfall, he noticed some shiny coins in the pool's sand: gold and Spanish silver coins. There might be more treasure in that cave that would require further exploration. Homer decided, on the spot, to name the cave after Gabriel. The coroner and the spelunker joined the archeologists, the tennis academy, Homer, Ludmilla, Sasha, Boris, Valentina, and Vladimir in a lovely lunch under the oak tree by the kitchen window. Everyone talked and told stories. Homer's mood lightened a bit as he sat by Dr. Gisler and talked about Monaco and the French Riviera—her home.

Homer's life had become exceedingly complicated, beyond his wildest imaginings, and yet he felt alive in a way he could not explain. The coming months would bring new twists as his new father pursued posthumous marriage to Homer's mother, Angelina. The wedding date was set for August in a cemetery just outside of Nice, France. Her exhumed remains were placed in a new casket and shipped to Nice while the story went viral on social media—an unusually romantic hit of the year! Leopold could see the writing on the wall and had a pleasant discussion with his cousin Armand. Leopold decided to leave the firm to pursue his real passion—making candid TikTok videos of wild animal stunts. He wasn't concerned about giving up dibs on a billion-dollar fortune as long as he had enough to live on and a fund for his video making. Armand had Archie make the arrangements, which he did with gusto.

Homer and Armand talked daily, and the Count made it official, at least in France and Switzerland, that Homer would be his legal, biological heir. When Homer removed his mother's casket to ship it to France for the wedding, the coroner took a small piece of her toenail, allowing further DNA testing. Homer and the Count were now a 99.9% match as biological father and son. Homer would inherit the company and keep both the historic family estate and the lake house in Switzerland.

Dr. Gisler and Homer talked and brunched every day as the site exploration progressed. She found some more Spanish coins in the ground around the cave, and a full investigation of the cave was planned for later in the fall. She also found a piece of granite with "1540" etched deeply into the stone. Dr. Gisler consulted other leading archaeologists. The consensus opinion was that the artifacts found my mean that the exploration of Georgia by Spanish explorer Hernando De Soto had gone further north than anyone had ever thought. But the Mayan pottery remained a mystery. One that required Dr. Gisler's continued presence in Grace indefinitely.

Deputy Historian Meeks and Chief Historian Lowman expanded

the Grace History Museum at Courthouse Square, preparing for a Smithsonian visit to see the unique "Mayans and Spanish in North Georgia" exhibit that would open in the fall.

Deputy Historian Meeks was also enjoying his courtship with "his little fibrillator" Connie Marlboro. Sally and Rev. J. Leland Jackson decided to open a campground up the road from Homer on Jasmine Mountain, where some of the best local mushrooms grew. The reverend would split his time between the Grace Church, where he was now the semi-retired pastor emeritus and a new ministry for weekend campers and mushroom pickers.

New Sheriff Dinsky hadn't made any significant mistakes on the job yet, and she talked with Mikhail daily as he progressed through his training in London. Valentina was, well, just wonderful Valentina. And Vladimir and his new friend, Jack, talked about engineering and maybe building more tennis courts in town. Carl decided to retire immediately as Mayor and Betty stepped in, at least temporarily. Lula Bell now had Carl all to herself, and he was kicking himself. But, she did let him drive his blue 351 to his daily golf outing. She just couldn't understand why it took him so long to get back home.

CHAPTER 28

FINAL REVELATIONS

With Homer's mother's mausoleum crypt vacated, Homer made arrangements with the aged, grieving, but now at peace, Alice Montcliff to have little Gabriel interred in the mausoleum. Alice was Gabriel's mother, the widow of Edgar Montcliff. Homer agreed to have Kipling's poem "If" returned to the original masculine form, and the name and dates changed to reflect Gabriel's short life. Homer called Alice regularly in Naples and promised her that he would make sure Gabriel's mausoleum was looked after.

After Gabriel's interment in the mausoleum in late July, Homer called Alice to give a quick update and let her know that he would be going to France for his mother's wedding and reburial.

"Homer, yes, I saw a story about Angelina on the news. Really romantic in a morbid sort of way. I wish I were able to do something like that," Alice said.

Homer paused. "Alice, I am not sure I understand. You were already married to Mr. Montcliff."

"Oh, Homer, I'm not talking about him. You know he was the father to the other six children, but Edgar was an absent, indifferent husband. He was gone most of the time. Business, traveling, affairs. Left me at the estate to tend to things."

"I am sorry to hear that, Alice," Homer replied, not yet grasping what it had to do with Gabriel.

"One summer, I took a little trip to the Cote D'Azur and had a fling. A handsome, younger Frenchman. We had a wonderful time. Sailing, climbing some of the local mountains. Long afternoons together. And nights. I was gone for a month. Edgar had a nanny for the children, and when I returned, I brought something back with me. Gabriel. He was born the next spring."

Homer was silent.

"Edgar stewed for years and eventually figured it out and had the man investigated. He was a member of a crime syndicate, a mafia family that had connections in Italy, France, Spain, and even Switzerland. So, we kept things quiet and never let on to anyone that there was an issue. But Edgar never accepted Gabriel. So, when Gabriel disappeared, he thought my lover or his associates kidnapped him. I didn't think so, but Edgar wanted no part of searching further. So, that's when we moved. The mills were going to close anyway, so it was convenient."

"Did Gabriel ever find out?"

"Not about his true father. He did find out about the mills closing and that we were considering moving. He was furious with us and kept talking about finding gold to save the mills so we could stay. Made no sense to Edgar or me. That boy had fantasies about bears in the woods and gold coins on the mountain behind us. He was a dreamer."

FINAL REVELATIONS

Homer's heart ached as Alice told all. He didn't say anything about the gold coins spotted in the cave. It would probably take quite a while to explore, and Alice might not be around by then. Nor did he mention the bear that he had heard as well. Now it was the figment of two boys' imaginations or maybe something real. But, Homer was curious about the Mayan pottery.

"Alice, thank you for sharing those intimate memories. I do have a question about the estate. We found a piece of old earthen pottery here, and I wonder if you know anything about that." Homer was vague, and Alice thought he meant a piece of pottery in the house.

"The Mayan pottery? Edgar had business dealings in Mexico. He was going to set up a textile plant down in the Yucatan at one point. Never happened. But, he made several trips down there and got very interested in the Mayans. Bought a lot of artifacts and had them shipped up to the estate. They were cheap back then. He lost interest after a while and just stacked them up out in the field near the workshop. We didn't take them with us when we left. You might look out in the field. There should be a bunch of that stuff out there."

Homer thought a moment before he answered. Dr. Gisler had a keen interest in the pottery and exploring Homer's estate for more. She had already hinted that she might need to stay in Grace for many months.

"Oh, we built some tennis courts out there and didn't find anything. Must have been hauled off."

"Well, I suspect it would be museum quality stuff now. Too bad."

ABOUT THE AUTHOR

Chesley Richards grew up in South Carolina and lives near Atlanta with his wife, daughter, four cats, and Mr. Pickles. A storyteller since he was ten years old, *Homer's Grace* is Chesley's first novel.

CPSIA information can be obtained
at www.ICGtesting.com
Printed in the USA
BVHW031155270922
648078BV00015B/431